ABLONG

ABLONG

A NOVEL

BY

ALAN SALANT

THE OLIVER ARTS & OPEN PRESS

Library of Congress Cataloguing-in-Publication Data
Salant, Alan, 1955–
Ablong: A Novel

ISBN: 978-0-9819891-8-1

The Oliver Arts & Open Press
2578 Broadway, Suite #102
New York, NY 10025
http://www.oliveropenpress.com

For Sheila

Now therefore... I shall apply myself seriously and freely to the general destruction of all my former opinions.

— Descartes, *Meditations*

ABLONG

BY ALAN SALANT

Dawn sun, after a night of rain, draws up water from puddles on nearby roofs and streets.

I've had murderous thoughts for days, and all the while I've been trying to detach myself from this plane of existence, though that's not why I'm starting this diary.

In the elevator a guy's reporting a new medical problem, people surfeited with culture, just exploding.

"What, like vomiting up paintings and stuff?"

"No," he says, and he's about to explain as I get out.

The next elevator ride, a grad student's vehement that grammar should tell us how to speak, not just describe how we actually speak.

"I like that it's descriptive," says his companion. "Like Aristotle."

"How is that like Aristotle?"

"Because Aristotle didn't say how things should be, simply went around figuring out how things are. How do we organize governments? What makes theater work? Who are we? What are we seeking?"

It's been a very peristaltic day for me, my hiatal hernia in all its glory.

I work for an elite Eastern university. I'm a professor. I had one brilliant idea that got me tenure and—years later when its medical implications surfaced—wealth and a Nobel Prize. I don't care for kids, adolescents least of all. The hiring committee wasn't worried.

"We're not recruiting you for your personality," the chairman said. My brilliant idea created a new field of study, so I get thank-you notes from academics who've put their kids through college on it.

I had the idea when I was 21, while I was sitting on the crapper.

I go five-six, one hundred sixty pounds. I have blue eyes, brown hair, a beard deciduous to the beat of my inner climate. I tell people that the scar across my forehead came from a fight in a bar, or sometimes I say it's a war wound, a guy knifed me in some imperialist jungle-fight. If they're not good in math maybe they'll think Vietnam.

I have a strange form of mystical experience. It happens only when I'm eating broccoli. When I'm eating broccoli my mind becomes different, and I seem to be in communication with people from another world, if it's even a world.

If I have seasoning on the broccoli they don't appear, though I can get away with a little salt. Then they just appear at an angle.

Yellow lamps along the street commemorate something. A guy's committing a misdemeanor in the trees, but if there's no cop to see it, was there a crime? In the sky two birds appear to be mating, one falls flat to the ground, plop. OK, maybe not mating. A sign from heaven, war on the horizon? A couple of students approach.

"How can you help me?" I ask politely.

"Shouldn't it be the other way around?"

"So you want me to help you?"

Students come up to me all the time, expecting something to rub off on them, wanting something from me, pretending that they want to give to me.

"No, we just wanted to say how much we admire your work."

"Oh," I say. "Thank you very much."

They had me on a talk show the other day to discuss the field I founded. I explained that it's the key to all knowledge. Old TV trick: make an outrageous statement and don't back down.

"What do you mean?" asked the host.

"It really does," I said. "It explains everything."

"How so?"

This is where it helps to read a lot.

"It's like Plato said." I shaped my face to its most sincere expression. "Knowledge isn't really knowledge 'til the whole thing's interrelated. Galileo too, and it was a big deal for him. Folks said you can't do physics with math, you can only do each subject by itself."

"So your idea is a way of interconnecting—"

"Exactly," I said.

"I'd really like to know more about this," said the host.

I'll bet he would.

It's not that I can't stand adolescents. Well, actually it is.

"Sorry," I call out. "Office hours are over."

"It says two to four Tuesdays." A coed.

"Exactly."

"It's three right now."

I'm sitting here, jotting on a yellow legal pad. I'm keeping this diary to mislead biographers. Already five writers have approached me, and I'm proud to say they've all regretted it.

"The sign doesn't say which Tuesdays, does it?"

There'll be a complaint from some parent, paid a lot of money, this is the kind of treatment my kid gets?

A flood of black evening douses the twilight fires on the rim of sky. I try gargling. It's been a rough day, and I haven't a clue why I'm having these murderous thoughts. Usually gargling would be helping by now.

Eventually I chew some broccoli. It's my LSD, except it really is broccoli. I don't know if it's a creative developmental choice of my digestive system, following orders other than mine, some evolutionary pilot project or rejected path from the past. I'm tested annually, check for cognitive holes, make sure the stuff isn't eating my brain. And I've tested the broccoli too, fed it to other people, to cattle, pigeons, cats. Nobody acts strangely under the influence except me—I mean, cats act strangely, but that has nothing to do with the broccoli.

I wish it was corn on the cob. Tasty.

What these guys inside the broccoli tell me is that we have to open our minds to a different universe. Well, telling isn't quite right. And they don't actually care what I think, but it's more like: you're watching a guy on a soccer field and he's sprinting and then suddenly he's flying fifty feet above the ground, becomes a bird.

Maybe it was the student who came up to me and said he'd decided I'd be his mentor. That was three days ago. Yes, I think that's it, that's why I'm so angry.

"It doesn't work that way," I said. "Mentoring's a choice of the mentor. It's like the spirit descending on you. You don't get to control it."

Alan Salant *Ablong*

"I heard that you've never helped anybody," he said.

I considered that for a moment.

"Probably true," I said, though there are those daily thank-you letters from academics. But that wasn't my intention. No harm, no foul.

He smiled.

"But what's your point?" I asked him.

"We're a perfect match," he said. "You never helped anyone, nobody ever helped me. We're both virgins."

"Surely your mom did something for you," I said. "Like gave birth to you or something."

"She tried to abort me," he said.

"Ah, like Cardan," I said.

"Sorry?"

If I explained that Cardan's *The Great Art* was the first modern math book, or that with the works of Copernicus and Vesalius it initiated the scientific age, he'd have something to go on.

He stared at me, awaiting an explanation.

"Well, gotta go," I said, and I walked away.

If it had ended like that, I wouldn't be having these homicidal fantasies. But the kid grabbed my arm.

"That's assault," I said, turning toward him.

"You need me," he said.

"I'm not kidding," I said.

I opened my cell phone and he let go of my arm.

"You're making the biggest mistake of your life if you don't become my mentor," he said. "And you know I'm right."

And he flicked his business card at my feet and walked away.

Before picking it up—and I did pick it up—I could smell flowers, deep wooded flowers, stakes of sunlight probing the ground through holes in leaves. I stuffed the card in my pocket.

A few years ago there was a murder in the philosophy department. It happened at a corporate-style retreat, only philosophers and the motivational idiot were in attendance. It was an experiment to see, well, something. The philosophers tried hard to get out of it, but the chairman felt that, yes, it had really come to this.

The dead man was the motivational idiot, found stabbed in the morning. So the suspects were all the philosophy professors.

"I'm surprised more of these motivational guys aren't killed," Jeanine tells me, Chaucer expert, we're discussing rumors of a possible break in the case. "It just seems like it would provide the right closure."

Through connections, I illegally got to see the tape of one interview.

"Even if we postulate that I was capable of it," said Erdenheim, phenomenologist, "I think we can exclude—"

"Gimme a swab from your mouth," said the detective.

"I'm a locus of rights," said Erdenheim.

"That's what they all say," said the detective, popping another Advil in his mouth. The detectives had a pool going, this guy's money was on the existentialist.

It's the next day. I dreamt of mermaids, unicorns, and love, woke with a bleeding lip.

Breakfast is burnt toast and eggs over easy. I smoke a cigar to aid the digestion and listen to the news where someone's trying to make sense of the entire world, explaining trends involving seven billion people, he doesn't even seem embarrassed, my kinda guy.

As best I can figure it, Burroughs was right, Pynchon was right, we live in a control system that's getting worse by the day, really could kill us all, and don't kid yourself, quickly if it wants.

I'm not as sure as Burroughs was that it involves insects. Actually, throw in Gaddis while you're at it—everything's a fake. I dreamt of a study that claims there's been nothing real in the Western world since about 1800, we're all Pinocchio.

I stare for a few minutes at a bottle of vitamins. I never take them, I just stare at them. Except for the hiatal hernia I haven't been sick in twenty years, low blood pressure, cholesterol right where it should be.

I nick myself twice shaving, then it's off to lecture hall. I'm writing this on my little portable, transferred the notes from the yellow legal pad.

From the podium I examine the coughing class, seems like everybody has some kind of bug. Two deans rejected my proposal to quarantine all the students in the condemned building at the end of campus.

Today I'm summarizing the history of Western philosophy from the perspective of the field I invented, which I insisted on calling Quantum Aerobics, though everyone else calls it Quantum Biotechnics. Its impact has been compared to that of the introduction of the concept of historical time. There are seventy departments of Quantum Biotechnics in the US alone, plus a few offshoots called Cognitive Biotechnics and now even something called Cognitive Micro-Biotechnics, academic

Alan Salant *Ablong*

splinter group, soon they'll be claiming credit for bombings.

Quantum Aerobics has been used to prove that quantum mechanics is a subsidiary of chaos theory and that Homer was a self-hating woman. The first development accelerated the genome project by a factor of twenty, that nervous system mapping by a factor of eighteen, and IBM's Blue Gene by a factor of eleven. The Homer one got some guy a publishing contract and he appeared on *Charlie Rose*. I'm skeptical. I got interviewed about it by *Classical Mediterranean World Quarterly*, told them the writer doesn't know his ass from his elbow. It's a phrase the reporter wasn't familiar with.

"Is that a cognitive deficit?" he asked. "A problem involving the mapping of body parts to brain?"

All right, the lecture's over, the same damn kid is staring me down in the hallway.

"I'll call the cops," I say.

He has a surly aspect. He looks me up and down, actually makes me nervous, must be a biological thing. Hate the way all the stuff that matters about me was probably created among beings who didn't speak, back in some jungle or ocean. I wouldn't have done it that way.

"You're supposed to be my mentor," he says.

"Whose supposition?" I ask.

"It's your purpose," he said. "Haven't you ever wanted to have a purpose?"

I have eighty million purposes in the bank, could have more if I wanted. And of course there's the broccoli.

"You ain't it, kid."

"We'll see," he says.

I notice he's got a gash on his arm, reminds me of the wounded cat a colleague took in. I brush past him in that way where you faintly touch a person, as if to say: you don't even exist.

"We'll see," he repeats, a little desperation in his voice. Ah, that means it won't happen.

Across the field, members of the Organic Chemistry survivor's group are holding hands. Ed Blumenthal's on my cell.

The fact that I've never helped anybody doesn't stop people from being in my life. I'm the father they had, the unresponsive one. People who had good fathers tend to have nothing to do with me, but you'd be surprised how many people had bad ones. And they just see me and figure they'll work their stuff out with me in the supporting role. A chick in Anthropology draws the offspring of narcissistic mothers.

6

Ed's an important guy in his field, whatever that is. I keep forgetting, and even when I remember I make a point of pretending I don't.

"Loved your article on frogs," I tell him.

"I'm not a biologist," he says. "My field is—" whatever it is.

I don't even have to pay attention. Folks want to co-write papers with me, get photographed with me. This could have been a real pain, but a while back I realized I could just keep being myself, not giving a damn about anybody else, and my life would go on as before.

I should mention that my idea was the basis for curing cerebral palsy, that was its first application. By now you can add Lou Gehrig's disease, Huntington's, eight cancers and counting. So when I say I haven't helped anyone, I mean one on one, person to person. I once dreamt of myself as the Industrial Revolution, no empathy and I cure people without lifting a finger.

"What's really up, Ed?"

Ed has long hair. As best I can understand it, Ed believes we were on the verge of big answers in the 1960s, turning over the soil of society, aerating, and he's doing his best to recreate the decade by his personal appearance.

"OK if I stop by?" he asks.

"Heck, sure," I say.

I like Ed, or more accurately, I like being with Ed. He's thin-skinned and I don't give a crap, and he takes it because of the father stuff. He doesn't realize that's what's going on, and I don't see why I need to tell him.

"I had an insight," says Ed.

"Really?"

"Statistically," he says, "the likelihood is high that somewhere in America is an individual who precisely embodies the core American character."

"That's an interesting observation," I say.

"That's not the insight," says Ed. "What I realized is that I might not get along with that guy."

"And?"

"Maybe I need to stop trying to change America, and just let it be itself. Maybe I'm doing harm by trying to make America into someone else, like a parent mutilating a kid."

"I do know a good barber," I say.

Beside an elm tree an enthusiastically bearded young professor is explaining the importance of literature to a skeptical brunette.

"My sister's boy," he says, "just turned eight. He hides flashlights around the room and writes stories under the covers at night after bed-time. The stories take my sister to the real places in his brain, things he'd never say, who he is."

"She snoops?"

The kid who wants me to mentor him spots me, comes over, I'm thinking order of protection.

"What do you have to tell me today?" he asks.

It's a good idea. Create the reality, make me think I must have something to tell him.

"It doesn't make sense to me," I say. Where's that coming from?

"What doesn't make sense to you?"

"The whole damn thing," I say. "It doesn't make sense to me, any of it. I don't know if there's a God, I don't know if there's something I'm supposed to be doing, I don't know anything."

"Lying won't work," he says.

"The strange thing is," I say, "I'm not lying."

For a balding guy in his mid-fifties whose face is cracking, I have quite a sex life. Woman like to screw Einstein, especially when he's willing, and this Einstein's willing.

So we're lying in bed, at 56 I've still got it, thank you Viagra. She's feeling smarter because she's just had me, and so she's going on about her dissertation and getting more and more animated about it. Something about how Proust's masterwork would have been different if his protagonist was an amnesiac.

"It's food for thought," I say.

"People think you're nasty," she says.

"And you know different."

"I know that a tender heart beats in there," she says.

I put my hand cautiously to my chest.

Ed's next visit, he's in a plaid shirt and blue jeans.

I've never understood plaid, boredom made pattern. If I ran the conspiracy to make the whole world gray, corporate, and dull—which seems to be progressing nicely—I'd make plaid the uniform. Like those carpets with geometric patterns that people spend tons of money on.

"I just can't get my head clear," says Ed.

"It could be all that hair," I say. "Have I mentioned that I know a

8

good barber?"

"I like my hair the way it is," says Ed.

"At least someone does," I say. "But tell me, Ed, what seems to be the problem?"

"I've just been thinking and thinking."

"About the frogs," I say sympathetically.

"I don't do frogs," says Ed. "I've told you that a million times."

"But you know they're dying, right?

"Who's dying?"

"Frogs," I say. "All the gender problems. You do read, right?"

"I was reading at a twelfth-grade level before my eighth birthday," he says.

"No, but I mean now," I say.

He's turning red, and he doesn't want to turn red because he believes he never gets angry. He believes he never gets angry because his parents rejected him whenever he was angry. He also believes he's a special being because he never gets angry. Right now he's really pissed.

"Why do you say stuff like that?" he asks.

"I don't know what you mean."

"Suggesting that I'm illiterate."

"Ah, don't take it seriously," I say, hoping he'll take it seriously. "A lot of people lose the ability to read."

"I've never heard that."

"There've been hundreds of articles about it," I say. "How could you have missed them? It goes back to my point."

He takes out a sheet of paper and jots a note. I know by now how this is going to go. He's writing that he has to check for those articles. Tomorrow he'll come back to me with the fact that there aren't any such articles in any academic database, and I'll tell him that I wasn't referring to reading per se.

He chuckles now, and jabs me on the shoulder. This is him pretending he isn't angry, because he just can't be.

"So you were saying something," I say.

"Yes," he says. "I just can't seem to get my ideas to fit together. There's—" and he launches into a long discussion. Once he's there, I can safely start munching on my broccoli. I carry it in my pocket for such occasions.

About twenty minutes later he finishes.

"So what do you think?" he asks.

"I'm not sure," I say. "I think you need more clarity."

"Yes," he says. "Clarity, that's what I need. That's it exactly."

Alan Salant *Ablong*

This night I'm alone, and it's a pleasant sensation. I feel myself expelling the world from myself yet again, all the influences of everybody trying to force me to be something, so much happened to our forebears on those ancient plains, in that ancient wood.

I tell people I've slept with eight thousand different women, that I'm the Wilt Chamberlain of the academic world. Jimmy from Statistics wants it as a histogram, how many from each continent, age distribution. I tell him that I have the data but it's un-collated, and give him sheets on which I had a pathologically eager grad student named Eugene let his imagination run wild.

"It's all in there," I say.

Jimmy misses a few departmental meetings, eventually emails me.

"It's astonishing," he says.

"What is?"

"It's a perfect bell curve," he says. "I have to apologize: I thought at first you made the stuff up."

I call in Eugene.

"What did you do?" I ask.

"I didn't want him to catch on," he says.

"How long did you spend on it?"

"I have a laptop and a good math program," he says. "Took me an hour."

"There are a few academic papers you could really help out on," I say.

"That's a terrible idea," says Eugene. About the sex thing he could look the other way, but basically he believes in truth, knowledge, the great effort since we stood up on two legs and began trying to figure out exactly what it is we're seeing from this vantage point.

"I don't see why," I say.

"Because it will corrupt the process. Garbage in, garbage out."

"It's self-correcting," I say. "The whole theory of errors says it'll work out, not only that, truth requires dishonesty or you won't have the right randomness, the data will cluster too closely to reality to be real."

"I don't think it works like that," he says.

"It's free-market principles," I say. "Mindless greed that destroys entire communities is the engine of progress. It all comes out in the wash. Best of all possible worlds."

"I'm not sure that's the idea behind the free market."

"Oh, that one I'm pretty sure about," I say.

Jimmy, though, won't let me alone. He's found a connection between the women I've been with and something involving the distribution of fish in the Aleutians, and it's too important for email.

"I didn't understand," he says, dragging a chair away from my table and sitting backwards, begins playing unconsciously with mustard packets from Chinese takeout, "until I saw your pattern. And then I was looking over some data about the fish, and it all became clear. They're not gonna like it."

"The fish?"

"No, the oceanographers' convention. It isn't good news, you know. The planet's in much worse shape than I realized."

Jimmy's agitated, almost falls over the front of the chair twice, so I offer him lo mein. But my words don't register. For the next hour he outlines all the things going on in the world ecosystem—he's statistical consultant to a half-dozen environmental organizations—while I begin munching broccoli from the refrigerator.

"So there you have it," he says finally.

"You make quite a convincing case," I say.

"Isn't it?" he says. "And we're doing it to ourselves, that's the worst part."

"Well, I don't know," I say. "It's probably preferable to having someone else doing it to us."

That gets him thoughtful.

"You might be right," he says. "You old rascal you. Eight thousand, huh?"

"Give or take."

"Actually, it's 8,028," he says. "Unless you're holding back on me."

"Maybe a half dozen since I sent the data," I say.

"Oh, I'll need that," he says, then winks and tilts his head toward the bedroom. "Got someone waiting in back there?"

"No," I say.

"So strange," he says, "that your sexual history relates so perfectly to the core ecological issue."

"So what you're telling me—"

"Sex is an eternal mystery," he says, subconsciously thumbing his copy of *Gravity's Rainbow* that he takes everywhere, Bible of his inner world. "It's Tyrone Slothrop all over again."

The next time the kid accosts me, I feel something different. It takes me a minute to identify it: ah, I'm actually curious about him.

"You realize I'm an asshole," I say.

"Yeah," he says. He's got a newspaper under his arm, article on the right side about how Quantum Aerobics has just conquered multiple

Alan Salant *Ablong*

sclerosis. Tested it first on pigs, I think. Maybe it was horses.

"So why should I be your mentor?" I ask.

"Because you're my father," he says.

We do the DNA tests, must've been a bad condom, I won't even read the letter from his mom. He doesn't look too much like me, his good luck. I assume I can buy him off.

"I don't think you understand," he says. "I'm not asking you to be my father. I'm asking you to be my mentor."

"You know that I've slept with over eight thousand women," I say. "Whoever your mother is, I doubt I remember her."

"I know your reputation," he says.

"I'm actually complex and sensitive," I say. "Whitmanesque, a bundle of contradictions. You lied to me about being a student, by the way."

"I never said I was a student."

"No, but you implied it."

"How did I imply it?"

"By not saying you weren't."

"There are many things I'm not that I didn't say," he says.

"There's still time," I say. "What sort of person aren't you?"

He thinks a minute.

"Well, I'm not a Roman centurion."

"Look," I say. "I'll write you a check, will seven figures do it?"

"You still don't get it."

"Yeah, yeah, you want me to be your mentor. What do you want me to teach you?"

"How not to give a crap about anything," he says.

I wake with visions of the Fertile Crescent, those ancient river civilizations. Some slouch, shame of his village, is getting nervous agitations, sees a faint image of what's coming, tries to express the feeling by music, pottery, how he defecates.

Broccoli for breakfast is not recommended unless it's putting you in touch with alien civilizations. If it can't be corn on the cob, couldn't it be Cheerios?

I'm not sure how the broccolites enter my brain, but they're there before my second bite. I don't even know if they realize I'm watching them. Sometimes they look in my direction, but I can't tell if they have a sense of purpose about it because their eyes are always filled with meaning. At least I think they're eyes.

I was wrong: this diary isn't to mislead biographers, I doubt I'll let them anywhere near this sucker. No, the real purpose—I feel it as I'm writing, didn't realize it 'til now—is to talk about the broccolites, the things I see them do. And maybe I lack the key concepts, the vocabulary, is that why I woke Babylonian, cells of my slumber trying to draw how it feels?

I've taken to calling my son 'Tex' because he says he's from Georgia so it's close enough. He has some kind of name but he seems OK that I'm not using it.

He came by a couple of days ago, stayed into the evening, fell asleep, now it appears he's living here.

"There's a book," says Tex, "that's always up-to-date." Georgia's in his inflections but the syntax and phrasing are TV-mainstream.

"What do you mean?" I ask.

"It was written long ago, but whenever you read it, it just feels up to date. It's like it moves forward with the times."

I wouldn't think much of it, except that I saw just such a book on my last broccoli trip.

"Do I talk in my sleep?" I ask Tex.

"I give up," says Tex. "Do you?"

I chew on my broccoli and I enter a strange room. It's a place of shapes, only shapes. Sometimes it seems that when the folks I'm watching turn at an angle to me, they too just become shapes.

I get meditative whenever I'm in that room. And this time I'm thinking how I have everything I need. Unfortunately I also have people around me, no matter what I do. I can be myself, and still there are people around me.

Tex is curious about me, pulls books off my shelf.

"Never understood space-time," he says.

"Me either," I say.

His eyes narrow.

"You wrote a book on it," he says.

"Doesn't mean I understand it."

"Seriously," he says. "Give me the scoop."

"I can lie," I say.

"Go ahead."

"You understand quantum, right?"

"No."

"Good," I say. "So if time is quantized, that means there are a finite number of moments—a whole lot of them, but finite. So you can take

Alan Salant *Ablong*

space—ordinary space with its three dimensions—and just stack copies of it on top of each other in a fourth direction."

"Where's the fourth direction?"

"At right angles to the other three."

"See, that's where I get lost."

"Yeah, me too," I say. "Think of it as one of those Dubai hotels but even taller, a stupendous number of floors, and time's the elevator except it only goes up. And memory's like gravity, within its field mind moves only down unless powered by extreme emotion or related forces."

"Sorry?"

"Ed's study of the literature shows a significant statistical correlation between precognition and powerful inner experiences such as the loss of a loved one," I say.

"Ed isn't here, what's the point?" asks Tex.

"Be a good son, make me some breakfast, don't go easy on the toast."

We have a system: when I'm entertaining, Tex goes elsewhere. That's the one rule I insist on: Dad gets to play.

"I don't really like it," says Tex.

"That's why God gave you a gullet," I say.

"What do you mean?"

"To swallow your feelings."

He exits, and a little while later I enter.

Susan hangs around 'til the next day, and we take a walk on the campus. She's sincere, so I can't resist.

"It's OK to work within the system," she says.

"It isn't," I say.

"You work within the system."

"I don't work," I say.

"You give lectures, you attend meetings."

"I get an exemption since I'm post-Christian. But 'til you make that leap, I think you're stuck with what Jesus said, all that love, and I fear that like our recent popes he'd be lukewarm at best about turbo-capitalism. I can help if you need to unload your worldly goods, including that McMansion."

She begins about the Reformation, the deep roots of the changes over centuries in Christianity, how everything evolves. I pretend not to listen and she finally storms off.

"You were pretty rough on her, dude."

I turn around to see a tall black guy, student who's shown up occasionally at my lectures.

"Lester," I say.

"Thomas," he says. "Close enough."

"Eavesdropping's a bad habit, Lester," I say.

"I'm still Thomas," he says.

"You'll always be Lester to me."

"I wasn't eavesdropping," says Lester. "Look where we are."

I look. The campus is a gossamer green dripping off trees waking from winter. Ivy buildings always give me an erection.

"What's your point?"

"You're out in the open," he says. "You're standing on a main walkway. A public space."

"It's university-owned land," I say. "So I don't think it can be called public."

"My point is, I wasn't eavesdropping."

"You've made a good career choice, Lester," I say. "You'll make an excellent lawyer."

"I'm majoring in ecology," he says. "But that's not important."

"I disagree," I say. "Ecology is very important."

"I mean—"

He stands flustered as I start to walk away.

"Hey," he says, catching up.

"Aren't you supposed to call me Your Honor or something?"

"We both know better than that," he says.

"Well, how about Herr Professor? I've long argued that we need more Germanic values in the mix."

"You were pretty rough on her," says Lester, looping back to the start.

"She had it coming."

"Why?"

My cell phone goes off. I'd say I was lucky, except I'd set it off by pushing a button.

"Yes," I say. "Oh, my goodness, I'll be right there."

"What's wrong?" he asks.

"I can't even begin to say."

Across a wide campus field, bouncing on buds of spring, a woman runs toward me to thank me. Her brother has cerebral palsy so he's going to be cured by Quantum Aerobics.

"It pleases me greatly," I lie.

"You are truly a wonderful man." She takes my hand and kisses it.

"I can't deny it," I say.

She hugs me but I don't hug back.

Alan Salant *Ablong*

"Thank you again," she says. I know she's looking for an emotional connection, wants to make contact with the one who changed her life, her brother's life, to feel he's knowable, part of her world. What about what I want?

The newspapers report that a few years ago an entire species apparently took a wordless vow of chastity and they're all dead. And its neighbor on the tree of life is imitating, rebuffs to all the gentleman callers, Lysistrata in the rainforest.

"It must be worrying the ecologists," I tell Jane. She's in Biodiversity. We're standing beside the Heart of Darkness School of International Affairs.

"To say that the ecologists are worried is to say that a fly captured in a spider's web is vaguely uneasy," she says. "The whole language of earth is changing to a strange dialect, words unfamiliar to the deep survival places in us all."

Pull up a chair, let's see what happens.

I visit the art museum. Bad luck: Lester's there.
"When does your cell phone go off next?" he asks.
"What are you talking about?"
"Everybody knows you push a button," he says.
"Everybody?"

I'm a kind of god on campus. One of the bad ones, the sort of god that used to be invented when life was really ghastly and people needed somebody in touch with the situation. Just having badness located in me makes people feel safer, like they've confined the problem to one place and can thus control it.

I tell my theory of religion to Bernard, or whatever name he's claiming to go by these days. Bernard's the Venti Grande Decaf Professor of Religious Studies. He said I'm not precisely right on some of the specific points. That's how he talks, respectfully.

"Which points?" I ask.
He looks unhappy, thinks a minute how to phrase it.
"Pretty much all of them," he says.
"You don't think that's why in old times they invented sadistic creepy gods?"
"I think it's more complicated than that," he says.
"I suppose you'll claim," I say, "that those gods were simply images of the creepy rulers of the time, as well as templates of the even creepier rulers that followed."
"I don't think I'll claim that," says Bernard.

Anyway, Lester's just staring at me.

"You thought you were fooling someone?"

"I did actually. But what's a law student doing in an art museum?"

"I wouldn't know," he says.

"I guess now I have to apologize for being rude," I say.

"Hey, I know who you are," he says. "And I admire you."

"Why?"

"I wouldn't have the guts to do what you do."

"I'm in a unique position," I say. "Against all intention I've helped so many people that I can do just about anything."

"But aren't you afraid?"

"Of what?"

"Of being such a sonofabitch."

"No," I say. "I wake up happy every morning."

"But doesn't it make you feel kind of alone?"

"I am alone," I say. "So are you. It's just that I admit it."

Dinner is spinach, cauliflower, a cheese omelet. I eat dairy but I won't eat meat, won't kill an animal, I'm like Hitler that way.

The phone rings as I'm swallowing the last bit of omelet. It's a young writer, he's researching a book on scientific creativity, wants to know how I came up with the idea of Quantum Aerobics. I explain about the crapper.

"No, but I mean the process," he says.

"You can read about that in any good anatomy book," I say.

It takes him a minute. "I don't mean the anatomical process."

"Oh," I say. "In that case, any good plumbing book."

"Poincare did it getting off a bus," he says.

"I've never done it getting off a bus," I say. "Or getting off on a bus, for that matter. Gotta go, sorry."

I open the refrigerator for my hit, a large stalk of broccoli with my name on it. At the first bite I see these beings just flying around, but on the second bite it's something I've never seen before.

Usually these guys are humanoid—a bit greener than your average human, but the same basic features. Not today. Today they've arranged themselves in a vast circle, and it's awfully familiar—they're blades of grass covering an enormous field. And then something that reminds me of a bio text, a picture of mitochondria.

Spring's opening all across campus, underground conspiracy, words whispered beneath the grass, up the tree bark, up the flower stems.

Alan Salant *Ablong*

The day after my third broccoli vision, when I was eight years old, I began noticing: everywhere there was a conversation going, one endless theater piece, you're in the audience, actor too, from the moment your consciousness switches on.

And even when it seemed earth was still, or the room was still, something was happening. And with this realization, at eight years old, I began to lose interest in pleasing people, they'll be here whatever I do, and once you create the form of something it keeps reappearing in other ways.

And that seemed fine to me then, but recently it isn't seeming fine, and maybe that's why I'm really writing this diary. Or perhaps I need more fiber.

I think I'd better write down the conversation I just overheard.

"So they drag Day into court," this guy is saying. Alpha male, sure, pre-law.

"Day as in: daytime?"

"Yep."

"On what charge?"

"Of being irrelevant to the human future."

"And?"

"The sheer pathos has everyone in the courtroom sobbing or on the verge. Day's wounded, infected, in pain. And the judge, in a yellow wig, just keeps calling out: 'Name?'"

"And what happens?"

"Finally Day turns to him. 'I go by many names,' he says, speaking through a trombone interpreter. 'Why have you called me into this place, to trap me in words?'"

"And?"

"The wall bursts open, liberator on a consulting basis arrived just in time. Hey, you going to the game tonight?"

"Yeah."

"Got time for a few beers after?"

That's the conversation I heard. I wish it wasn't, but it was.

A dream in which I'm screaming someone's name at the top of my lungs and a crowd is gathering around me. Except that apparently it wasn't a dream.

They admit me to a mental facility, put me under observation, give me meds that actually do calm me down.

I've kept it a secret all my life that I have this special relationship with broccoli. Do I let them know? Are these people seriously out to help me? I mentally review the history of psychiatric theories and facilities. Yeah, doubt it.

The doctor introduces himself with a cautious smile.

"I'm Dr. Benway," he says.

"You're not the Dr. Benway, are you?" I ask.

"I suppose I am," he says, puffs up a bit.

"I take it you've never read any Burroughs."

"I'm sure you believe it's possible for a person to read a burrow," says Dr. Benway in a hyper-rational voice.

"Why am I here?" I ask.

"You were rolling on the grass screaming at the top of your lungs: 'I am the Batman, I am the essence, I am the Batman.'"

Was that me? Right, the dream that wasn't. But Batman? Oh, wait: my memory of my voice resolves. It was Atman. Hindu.

"Maybe I was saying Atman," I say.

"Why would you say that?"

"I guess that's your job, doc, to find that answer."

A slothful slumber, not a single dream I remember, what are you doing in there, guys? What if the neurons unionize, demand better working conditions? I like being boss of this body, this being, whatever I am, that I had nothing to do in creating and will fight to the death to defend.

Or what if the nerve cells develop issues, neurotic neurons, the far shore of the synapse starts to look just a little too much like death?

Out the window it's rain as far up as I can see. I imagine my way past the rain, above the clouds, into deep space, across the universe. Maybe that's where my guys are.

A few weeks ago, some prick of a student told me that I'm guaranteed heaven for all the people I've cured, don't worry about getting bounced because I'm such an asshole, I think he did it as performance art. And what about my genocide against disease, do you lose points for harming, say, polio?

Bud from literature is here too. We meet in the cafeteria.

"What are you in for?" I ask.

"Oh, it's an experiment," he says. "I have to teach Ken Kesey next term, and I want to know what he's talking about first-hand."

"Is that true, or is it just part of your hallucination?"

"I'm pretty sure it's true," he says. "The creamed spinach isn't bad,

Alan Salant *Ablong*

by the way."

"So how long do you stay?"

"Three weeks," he says. "Then my wife and I have a cruise to Antarctica."

"You don't have a wife," I say.

"You've met her many times," says Bud.

"I'm just testing you," I say.

"And you?"

"I'm not married," I say.

"I mean, what are you here for?"

"I've been hearing strange conversations," I say.

"Well, you are attached to the math department."

"Stranger than that," I say. "I'm wigging out a little."

"Well, I hope they can help you. Anything I can do, let me know."

"Can you change the world around so that I'm the sane one? It isn't me that's crazy, it's the world."

"That's been tried," he says. "It tends to get bloody."

"Let me ask you this," I say. "Aren't words important?"

"You're asking a literature guy?"

"And when people say crazy things, aren't they really saying who they are? Isn't normal conversation just a ruse, societal glue, corporate fiction?"

"Who've you been reading?" he asks suspiciously.

"No, I'm serious," I say. "Don't we speak a censored language, and if we were being truthful we'd be talking all the primal urges?"

"You aren't OK, are you."

"Why, what I'm saying is crazy?"

"No," he says. "It's just that you sound sincere. That's worrying."

"But what I'm saying—"

"Look," he says, "I think the bulk of conversation is a lie of omission. My parents spoke comfortable lies all day, the world was too much for both of them. It's why I got into the lit racket. Tired of all the ways that war is peace."

"You're not going to do well in your career, are you?"

"Is it that obvious?"

I've been demanding visitors, not that I actually want to see anyone, but it's part of unsettling Dr. Benway who keeps saying he's not sure I'm ready yet. So I've been accusing him of planning to keep me committed and to file papers that I'm incompetent so that he can take my money. I tried it just as a gambit but it made him nervous, something's there, so I kept at it.

"How can I prove to you that I'm not doing that?" he asks.

"Sunlight's the best disinfectant," I say.

"I'm not sure that's true," he says. "They sell some over-the-counter stuff that's pretty damn powerful."

"What I mean is, let some people come by to see me. Throw open the workings of this entire hellhole, this chamber of horrors."

"Do you believe you're in a chamber of horrors?"

"Don't you? My own doctor's trying to rob me of all my money."

That gives me an idea.

"Listen people," I say, raising my voice, "you know who I am and that I have a lot of money, this guy won't let me have visitors."

We're raised to scam the other guy and blame him if he falls for it—I remember that sick feeling the first time someone said you must never be a sucker, folks are always looking to put one over on you—so it's just too believable for people not to believe it, and Dr. Benway knows.

"Hey, Pops," says Tex, visitor number one. He doesn't seem nervous at all. I expect nervous from visitors to the loony bin.

"You seem quite comfortable here," I say. "Like you fit in, belong."

"That's very paternal of you," he says.

"Aren't you going to ask me what I have to tell you today?"

"That didn't go so well last time."

"It took me to the next level," I say. "So roll the dice, let's find out what's the next level after this place."

It occurs to me that the next level has to do with broccoli and I miss it, however good the creamed spinach is.

"You seemed really upset," says Tex. "It was a little scary."

"Pardon my psychotic break," I say.

"You're—" He catches himself.

"Oh, say it."

"I'm supposed to be nice to you in here."

"I wouldn't be, if the situation was reversed."

"You wouldn't come at all."

"Fair enough," I say. "Did you bring the stuff?"

I've asked him to bring a little reading.

"Here Pops," says Tex, hands me *Madness and Civilization* and the *Myth of Mental Illness*. On discharge I'll present them to Dr. Benway with inscriptions.

"So what do you want of me?" I ask.

His eyes get cagey. Heck, he wants everything. The whole father

Alan Salant *Ablong*

experience.

"Let me guess," I say. "You want to know I'm OK so you can feed at the father-tit. Get confidence, masculinity, have a beer together."

"Father tit?"

"The male tits are there for a reason, but—and this isn't spoken of very often—nature's showing signs of at least early dementia, just plain forgot why it put them there."

He grabs a chair and pulls it bedside.

"I'd like to think there's really somebody in there," Tex says, pointing to my head.

"Oh, I'm here," I say.

"I mean, I want to make contact."

"There's an entire song about that. Can't always get what you want. Can't always get what you want. Can't always get what you want."

Dr. Benway's looking particularly cheerful this morning. He has something green in his teeth, right in front.

"You've got something right there," I say, pointing.

I watch him hesitate between checking and saying "I'm sure you believe I do." He decides to check, which I take as a sign I'm getting out soon.

"Still there," I say.

He jabs the finger around, keeps just missing.

"Still there," I say.

He walks to a mirror, gets it.

"Still there," I say. Can't help myself, a faint thought that it's about denial, I have to prove to myself I'm in control even if it's self-destructive.

"No, it isn't," he says, but he's puzzled, goes back to the mirror.

"Just pulling your leg, doc."

"If we let you out," he asks, "do you think you'll start screaming about Batman again?"

I'm guessing he's unconsciously eager to get me out of there.

"Atman," I say.

"Have you met this Atman?"

"Every day," I say.

"Hmm."

"Look doc," I say, "Atman is a Hindu term. The true self, the world-soul, the life-principle."

"What else is on your mind?" he asks.

"I recently read an interpretation of the Frankenstein story," I say. "How it's a symbol for the Industrial Revolution, proletariat from across Europe robbed of its roots, parents, origins, orphaned of their past, decapitated like the recent victims of the guillotine and then stitched together and pressed into service of the new industrial state."

He looks at his watch. "Can we expect more screaming?"

Right now I need to play his game, get out, but if I say I won't scream again and then I get out and scream again, how do I get out the next time? A novel idea occurs to me.

"I think I'm OK," I say. "I don't really know what made me scream that day, so I can't be sure. But I'll take it easy for a while."

Yeah, the truth. Try that, see what happens.

"All right," he says. "Your son has agreed to look after you. It's important that you keep taking your meds. Your son will look after that too."

Let me see if I can figure out Tex's angle. Take care of Dad, form a relationship. Good luck.

"So what were you thinking that day?" Tex asks. "When I asked."

A dull sensation, the kind of deep pain that says something's really wrong, rises in me. Oh: it's what I felt that day.

"Something about how nothing fits," I say. "Should I start screaming again?"

"Let me get popcorn first," he says.

"How come there's no such thing as momcorn?" I ask. "Gender bias, no?"

"What do you mean by 'nothing fits'?"

"I have a theory," I say. "The brain works on a problem, and the problem gets more and more general, until one day it applies to the whole universe and you try to answer it at that level, and then you're insane."

"And that's what happened that day?"

"I don't know," I say. "Really, I don't know."

I've had it all figured out, and now I don't. Is it possible I'm stuck being myself? Hey, that's not fair. I never signed up for this.

"And this is new to you?" asks Tex.

I didn't realize I'd said that last part aloud.

"Some switch has gone off," I say adjusting my underwear, it's all I'm wearing, "and now I'm worrying about this stuff. If I stop thinking about whatever set the switch off, I'll be fine."

"Could you maybe put on some more clothes?" he asks.

I get up and put a robe on. I'm feeling defeated, can't remember the last time I did anything anyone else asked just because they asked

Alan Salant *Ablong*

it. In the nuthouse I did stuff but that's because of a threat if I didn't. What's the threat here? Oh, abandonment.

I flip open a magazine, it's an analysis of the world, guy seems uneasy about Pakistan going Taliban with nuclear weapons, game theory was developed for two players and they often had the names "United States" and "Soviet Union," it gets complicated when you have more, cool.

"So," I ask, "you gonna hit me up for money, Tex? Expecting to receive the family coat of arms? What's the plan here?"

"I want to make my own life," says Tex.

"Then go to it," I say.

"But you're part of that life," he says. "I have to work out my father stuff."

"Genetics is a bitch," I say. "But I'll tell you my secret. Have one big idea and the rest falls into place."

"That worked for you," he says. "Not sure I'll be as lucky."

"It isn't luck," I say. "It's the power of positive thinking, coupled with regularity of the bowels. Did I ever tell you why Rome really fell?"

Tex burps.

"That burp proves my point," I say.

"You know, Pops, there's stuff you say that I really don't understand."

"Me too," I say.

"I'm saying stuff you don't understand?"

"Not you, me."

"I'm saying stuff I don't understand?"

"No."

He gets his logical circuits working. What's left?

"Oh," he says. "You're saying stuff you don't understand."

"Exactly," I say.

Safest course is to ignore that, and he does.

"Can you say more about the brain and its problems?"

"Very early," I explain, "we have problems to solve, and we go about trying to solve them, often without words or the assistance of higher brain functions because it's too soon, our neurons create decision paths in this premature environment. And as we grow up we keep trying to solve those problems without knowing why."

"Because they precede the maturing of the conscious mind."

"Exactly."

"What did you mean about broccoli?" asks Tex.

A dream: the sky's a vast question-mark over all existence. As a joke they don't understand, meteorologists on TV start wearing shirts with question-marks, seven-day forecasts with symbols no one can decipher, and their happy talk's sprinkled with an unnerving number of references to death. The traffic part's still OK, three-car collision on Route 1, take alternates.

I guess a thorough self-analysis would begin on the savannahs or the deep woodlands, wherever the human form took shape. Or you wander further along the genetic tree, get all genealogical, be the ape. Or further still...

Notepad in hand, his patient sinking into the couch, the analyst asks:

"So how did it feel to be a one-celled being?"

"Can't really say, doc."

"That's just resistance", says the analyst. "Here's the name of a support group for getting in touch with your inner amoeba, if not there's hypnotherapy, and they've done interesting things lately with lobotomies."

In his spare time Dr. Benway would stare at a panel with lots of knobs—gravitational constant, all the parameters of the physical world. And he'd start fine-tuning, and everything would change.

No, that wasn't Benway, that's my broccolites.

People are coming by, and I'm introducing them all to Tex.

"I'm his son," says Tex.

"Since when?" asks Lester, stopped by to see how the mighty have fallen.

"Since the sperm hit the egg," says Tex.

"Oh, a real son."

"Yep."

Lester looks at me for confirmation and I nod faintly.

"You must be so proud," says Lester, managing to look at both of us at the same time. Tex doesn't seem to know how to take that one.

"You've made Tex uneasy," I say.

"Your name really isn't Tex, right?" asks Lester.

"Ah, hell," says Tex. "How long 'til you start thinking like a Lester?"

Later that afternoon they fall into conversation, head to a bar. Great, an alliance.

Ed comes by in his plaid. He's having trouble, fun for me. Since I'm Dad, suddenly he's got competition, sibling rivalry, and on top

Alan Salant *Ablong*

of it he has to pretend he likes Tex because somewhere deep down Ed knows the real game, and if he gets angry at Tex his cover's blown. And of course Ed's not allowed to get angry anyway.

Tex is munching on a sandwich in the kitchen.

"So what part of Texas are you from?" Ed asks him, smiling in a way nature never intended. I'm watching to see if a few molars might drop out from Ed's facial tension.

"Savannah," says Tex.

Ed's smile gets even more unnerving.

"I didn't know Texas had a Savannah."

"I vaguely remember hearing there's a planned community," says Tex, helping a brother.

"But you're not from it."

"No."

"Ask Ed about his frogs," I suggest helpfully.

"You have frogs?"

"No," I say, "he studies them. His specialty. He's trying to figure out why they're dying all over the planet."

"That's interesting," says Tex.

"I don't study frogs," says Ed.

"No need to be embarrassed," I say. "Ed's parents wanted him to go into plankton."

"Someday I'd love to talk about frogs," says Tex. That's my boy.

"I agree with Ed," I say. "Modern science is a beautiful thing. It heals the sick, answers our questions, asks new ones that are simply, let's be honest about it, fascinating."

"I never said anything like that," says Ed.

"Sure you did. The day you complained how the Web's too Modern-centric, how we need an Internet devoted to content from the year 1200. How to sign up for the next Crusade, prayer schedules for your town, fashion tips for the peasantry, what to serve when the feudal lord comes by to sleep with your wife."

"It doesn't make sense," says Ed. "The whole idea of the Internet depends on a sequence of ideas that didn't exist in 1200."

"I'm saying, if they had the technology. I think that's implied in what you suggested."

"It's not just the technology, they didn't have the underlying concepts, entire memes that hadn't been formed—"

I nod enthusiastically.

"My bookie," I say, "got drunk once and said if he could figure out a way to make it practical he'd be taking 3:2 odds that modern science will mess everything up big-time."

26

"That's not what I was saying," says Ed.

"If it was, there'd be no need for me to say it."

"But you're nodding as if you agree."

"I am agreeing," I say. "Just not with you."

"You've got to tell me about the broccoli someday," says Tex. "Might as well be today, Pops."

I'm trying to figure the kid out. Galactic nerve to plant himself in my home, ignore every signal I give—well, I can see where he gets that from—and wait. I have a stray thought that only someone who never knew home would have such nerve, the desperation beneath it. Wait: Tex had a home. Oh, but I didn't.

"You wouldn't understand," I say.

"Do you understand?"

"Not really," I say.

"So it's like father, like son."

"Suppose I tell you a story," I say. "We'll say it's about a guy named Strauss. In other words, it's not about me."

"Sure."

"This guy Strauss has his first experience with broccoli when he's eight. He's chewing it, and like any normal kid he doesn't like it. And then suddenly he's seeing things as if there's a different eye in his brain."

"Like a third eye."

"Maybe a fourth eye," I say. "The third one's already taken for other purposes. It's as if there's this extra eye inside his brain that's showing him a different place."

"OK."

"So this guy Strauss excuses himself from the table, goes to his room, closes his eyes—"

"Closes his regular eyes."

"Right. And just sits there on his bed. And he's seeing stuff that isn't even in focus, he doesn't know what it is."

"Then what?"

"The next day there's leftover broccoli, back to his room, still blurry but a hint of an outline, like he's watching this whole nervous system forming, connecting. And a few days later, when it's broccoli again for dinner, he sees something a little clearer."

"What is it?"

"It's a humanoid, staring right at me, but not clear if the humanoid really sees me."

"You mean Strauss."

"I don't think the humanoid's named Strauss."

Alan Salant *Ablong*

"No, you're Strauss."

"Oh, right. The scene recedes and it's a whole group of them and in the center is, well, the universe. Galaxies in a circle and inside the circle is all of existence. And Strauss is just seeing it."

"But if the galaxies are the circle and existence is inside it, then the galaxies are really outside—"

"It isn't standard logic," I say. "Outside, inside. And I get this feeling, like if I understood the relationship between them and this thing in the center, I'd—well, I'd solve something I need to solve."

"You mean Sartre."

"Strauss," I say.

"Sorry."

"Keep up, OK?"

"But you've arbitrarily chosen the name." says Tex. "Like choosing the variable in an equation, it doesn't matter if you use s or t."

"This can serve," I say, "as a parenting moment, a teachable moment. Take my word for it son, it matters."

"That's the parenting moment? 'Take my word for it?'"

"Exactly," I say. "Can we consider the issue settled?"

"They're just names," says Tex.

"But by convention one stands for space, and the other for time."

"I thought Einstein showed that space and time are synonyms," says Tex.

"What the hell has your mom been teaching you?" I ask. "Anyway, if Levi-Strauss understood the relationship—"

"I thought he was just Strauss."

"Sorry. If he understood the relationship, he'd be able to do more than understand—something beyond understanding, a new kind of knowing, because understanding's spatial."

"You stand under something," says Tex. "You understand."

"Whereas this comes from a different etymological tree, it's something else entirely. But what gets me is that I see these damn humanoids and maybe I'm the only guy that's ever seen them, and maybe they wouldn't be happy if they knew I was seeing it, or maybe they've chosen me."

"It sounds like the Illuminati," says Tex.

"I'm not sure it does," I say.

"Sure," says Tex. "Illuminati, the Tristero, all those guys that secretly run the world. I think they're in it together."

"The Tristero's actually fictional," I point out.

"That's the secret of it," he says. "They're so out of sight that they only exist in a work of fiction. That's deep undercover."

The campus Thought Police come in to visit me the next day, three professors from my department and a couple of deans to quantify exactly how nuts their guy has gone to three decimal places. I insult each one in turn, then look for a way to insult them all collectively.

"Aren't you ashamed how our university is failing?" I ask.

"How so?" asks the most serious dean.

"In the 1950s we wasted an otherwise perfectly good decade craving security through conformity. And why? Because we'd glimpsed the abyss of recent depression and war, and, as you five know from personal experience, when you stare into the abyss, the abyss stares back at you."

"So?"

"Well, look around you." Make it as vague as I can.

"I guess he's OK," they agree as they leave.

I pick up my copy of *Remembrance of Things Past* which I'm reading backwards one paragraph at a time like playing an album backwards, on the lookout for other meanings.

I think we're all curious what happens after we die: boxers stopping fights mid-round to discuss it, brokers putting customers on hold on the trading floors. A new Euclid may unite all supposed facts about the afterlife into an interconnected logical system, and if he does?

I pose that question to Ed the next time he comes by plaidly.

"That's an interesting question," he says, looking furtively around to see if his sibling rival's in. "There'd doubtless be a vast number of contradictions. You can't build a Euclidean system on that."

"Godel said any system of sufficient complexity is gonna have its problems," I say.

Ed, who wants order in the universe, is displeased.

"I think Godel's over-rated," he says. "And Heisenberg."

"Absolutely," I say.

"So you're skeptical about their conclusions too."

"Skeptical? Not in the slightest. But they're definitely over-rated."

My first lecture back since insanity draws a large audience to see if the guy breaks down right in front of them.

"Why do you all hate America?" I begin.

Puzzled looks.

"OK," I continue, "open your hymn books to page 23."

I begin reading a hymn from something Pentecostal. A trio of deans get up from their seats in the front and come toward the lectern.

Alan Salant *Ablong*

"No, it's all right," I say. "How many of you came to see if I'd crack up again? Don't be shy, you all know. Hands."

Lots of hands.

"Now applaud yourselves for your honesty."

Lots of applause.

"Thanks," I say. "Today's topic is Quantum Aerobics and its Antecedents."

The deans exchange glances, back away from the stage, take their seats. Soon I'm talking about the night in 1619 when Descartes, by the Danube, dreamt for all Europe, saw a geometrized universe, his mission in life, the modern mind.

"I heard your lecture," says Tex. "I like the way you brought it all front and center."

"I couldn't stand the energy in the room," I said. "It was like one giant bad body odor. Had to do something,"

"The thing I didn't get," says Tex, "is whether you really believe that Anaximander and Archimedes and Boethius were antecedents, or if you just basically picked up the equivalent of a historical phone directory and took names at random."

That was eerie because one of my projects as a kid, rainy afternoon, was exactly that: I made a phone directory with the names of all the dead famous people I could think of. Was it being communicated in the way I dressed, scents my body released, patterns of my speech? How come Lobachevski and Bolyai and Gauss all had the same idea at the same time? And what about those UFOs people keep seeing?

"I wouldn't engage in academic fraud," I say. "I'm hurt that you'd think so."

"You aren't really hurt, are you?"

"It's just an expression. But in principle..."

"But Kierkegaard? Really?"

"I'll admit," I say, "that Kierkegaard is open to interpretation."

"I thought it was a brilliant talk," says Dean Wager, low man on the dean totem pole, who has to make the peace offering. We're sitting in my office, I offer a joint on which I've written 'this is not weed.' With broccoli meeting my basic alternate-reality needs, I don't smoke. The stuff's only here to annoy visitors.

"I gave it up for Lent," he says.

"This is not weed," I say, reading the reefer.

"There's evidence by the way," he says, "that Quantum Aerobics may be useful in treating Parkinson's."

I'm delighted that he calls it Quantum Aerobics. He's really sucking up.

"I know," I say. "Ever been to Manaus?"

"No," he says. "Do they have a lot of cases of Parkinson's?"

"Not that I know of."

"Interesting though that you mention Manaus," he says.

"Why?"

"Ever been to the Australian Outback?"

"I've been to Outback restaurants," I say. "Great fries. Didn't Manaus used to be in Brazil?"

"Still is," he says. "I'm thinking of taking a walkabout."

"In Manaus?"

"In Australia. My sabbatical's coming up. I need to get out of here."

"That's very un-Dean-like," I say, "and I worry what the other deans will think, the other arbiters of the cerebral process."

"Ah heck," he says, "I'm my own man."

I know this one. I've brought out this side in him. Put it back in, quick.

"I think that if you went on a walkabout it would be very uncool," I say.

"Why?" he asks, looks alarmed.

"Just very, very uncool," I say.

He frowns and gets up and walks out.

A three-year investigation and suddenly a break in the case, they know who killed the motivational idiot. Rumor that the chairman tried to suppress the result: as long as the killer wasn't known, departmental courses were jammed since it could be anybody.

"It was the Hegelian, right?" I ask Tex, who brings the news. "Tell me it was the Hegelian."

"Nope, not that Hegelian," he says.

"Oh come on, it had to be the Hegelian."

"Not the Hegelian."

"Then the neo-Platonist," I say. "Should have known, the damage those guys have done."

"Not the neo-Platonist," says Tex.

"The post-structuralist?"

"Nope."

"Oh wait, I know. It was the de-ontologist, he used to be a consequentialist before his breakdown. I never thought he fully recovered."

"It's not him," says Tex.

"Well who then?"

"You give up?"

"Yes, I give up."

"It's the phenomenologist."

"Which one? Jones or Higmanstoff?"

"Higmanstoff."

"What was his motive?"

"They don't know."

"What do you mean?"

"He confessed, he explained everything, but nobody could understand a word."

Inside the broccoli, I've resumed, there's a wild party at the universal center, flipping galaxies like Frisbees, pancakes, stuff I never wanted done to any galaxy I'm part of—and as they do it something changes in me, in the cosmos, how do we know our whole universe wasn't just revised by these galaxy-tossing humanoids? That the yesterday we imagine is different from the yesterday we imagined a few moments ago. I mean, do the math.

I want to tell Tex about it, it's making me a little nervous. Is it fair that we come into a world we don't know, and all the categories are up for grabs?

He notices my brooding, comes up beside me and puts a comforting hand on my shoulder.

"What's eating you?"

I think of naming all the microorganisms.

"It's a conversation I don't really know how to begin," I say.

"My motto is—"

"You're way too young to have a motto," I say.

"You know, you're a real asshole," says Tex.

"I do."

"I mean, you're about to open to me about something, you obviously want someone to talk to, and look how you treat me."

When the kid's right, the kid's right.

"All right, look," I say. "I saw something about the broccolites that makes me fear they might be up to no good."

I tell him about the flipped galaxies.

"Maybe it's a bad batch of broccoli," says Tex.

"I don't think you're taking me seriously," I say.

"Sorry," he says. "I just can't tell if you're playing one big practical joke on me."

"I'm not," I say. "I'm actually leveling with you. Suppose each of us leads a remarkably separate existence, and to hide the terror of that separateness we've invented language and culture—"

"To pretend we're all experiencing the same thing."

"Haven't you wondered why we really put artistic designs on our pottery? And Big Brother's a wish-fulfillment dream, total thought-control and uniformity so we don't feel so alone."

"And your point is?"

"My point is that the mark of my separateness is my broccoli hallucinations, which make me more apart from other people than any asshole stunt I could conceive. Should I be doing something about it when the great grooves of the universe are dissolving and there won't be any more music?"

"You're not having another breakdown, are you?" asks Tex.

"I actually don't think so," I say.

A mid-spring snowstorm has made a mess of everything, Canada sent it, need to tighten that border crossing. Early spring storms I understand, drive optimistic flowers to early graves since they're unfit for this world of disappointment. What kind of flowers do you bring to that particular funeral?

"Earth's turning on us," says one student cheerily to a girl he's trying to impress.

A lot of the chitchat across the white campus is about the unpredictability of the planet, and though these kids are young I detect a tinge of hysteria. Their parents keep promising that things don't really change, each generation repeats the experience of its predecessor, all pretty stable if predictably depressing, world without end. And yet these kids aren't sure. Are we-the-faculty supposed to be doing something about that?

On my way to the library, I run into Ed in the snow talking to an admiring female.

"Are you taking Ed's new course?" I ask.

Ed rolls his eyes.

"Ed, you have a new course?" she asks.

"Yes," I say. "It runs four years. Ed reconstructs what's really going on at a given moment, as opposed to what we think is going on. He shows the place our actions come from, where they look quite different from the actions themselves."

"Interesting."

"Using every medium known to humanity," I say, "Ed shows step by step the formation of our minds to the point where we have the shock of recognition at almost every moment. He completely dismantles us in search of the mental equivalent of the quark. And as

Alan Salant *Ablong*

you sit in his class you feel yourself decomposing—"

"It sounds frightening."

"I can only say that from what I've heard, and I admit I don't hear everything, Ed's students experience it as orgasmic. And they're amazed that what seemed solid was a gluing together of parts. How do you put it, Ed? 'As if a full blue afternoon sky could be separated into segments.' And to recreate that prototypical mind Ed encourages a night of drunkenness, hence the required purchase of a beer bong."

"Why haven't I heard about this?"

"I for one am surprised," I say. "But the theme is that one can take oneself as one is, focus on the tasks and problems that one's body presents, take them as gospel."

"Or?"

I'm impressed that she realizes there's an 'or'. Suppleness of mind, what's she like in bed with that lithe mentality?

"Yes," I say, "the first approach is like obeying a shouting tyrant. But instead one can ask why one thinks as one does and whether alternate approaches are possible, viewpoints from which other actions would spring."

"In other words, the part that says I must—"

"That part can be questioned if you choose. And the part of oneself that most urgently says 'this is who I am' is the part most to be questioned, since the urgency's an indicator that it's imposed from outside or born in our early desperation."

"But isn't the urge sometimes a joyful and genuine inner assertion of life?"

"Yes," I say. "Ed perhaps goes too much to an extreme."

"None of this has anything to do with me," says Ed.

"To the contrary," I say. "It has to do with all of us."

Ed rolls his eyes again and looks up toward the heavens while nearby a heated argument erupts over whether an adult whose parents die can be termed an orphan and whether Orphan-Americans could gain traction as a new interest group.

Night. I take the broccoli to see what my friends at the center of the universe are up to. I could swear one of them's staring straight at me with a knowing look in his eyes, but then he turns away and when his head's at an angle to me it vanishes. The galaxies look like a giant candle-flame.

"I heard that Quantum Aerobics may hold the key to curing epilepsy," says Lester.

"I didn't hear that one," I say. I flip on the computer and head to the Fans of Quantum Aerobics website. Sure enough, the twelve-year who runs it has linked to an article about epilepsy.

These things are coming up fast now. They're not even doing clinical trials anymore, just give the treatment to a handful of people and if it works start mass-producing. Ninety-nine percent cure rates, it would be a hundred except there are always the outliers, genetic hinterlands.

The phone rings.

"How does it feel to be Pasteur and Salk and Sabin all wrapped up in one?" asks a pretty, female voice.

"You mean about the epilepsy," I say.

"Yes," she says.

"How did you get my number?" I ask, hanging up.

The snow forms a cold rectangle around my house. Kids are throwing snowballs and one of them almost cracks a window. I've never been as good at spooking kids as I am at spooking adults, so this won't be so easy. I put on my game face.

"There's a dead man in here," I say. "Please respect the dead."

One of the kids looks uneasy, but the other guy's just smirking.

"There's nobody dead in there," he says.

"You don't know what you're messing with," I say, and this time I've gotten his attention. I thought of the broccoli people and it got conveyed.

"Hey," he tells his friend, "maybe we should get out of here."

The guy that invented logarithms went around in black capes and freaked out the neighbors. Maybe he knew something; there's a lot to learn from the history of math.

"You told me but I forgot," says Lester, talking to Tex. "How did you know this gentleman was your Dad?"

Ed comes by. I decide to trip him up.

"How are you feeling today?" I ask.

"You want to know?"

"Yeah, I do."

"You really want to know?"

"You bet."

He tells me, and I keep pumping him with questions, and pretty soon we're in that territory where you really shouldn't be telling anyone this, Ed.

"In the quiet before sleep," he's saying, "I've found that my mind

Alan Salant *Ablong*

has recently gained the ability to do what I call emotional exercises."

"I'd like to think I've had something to do with that," I say.

"I doubt it," says Ed.

"What are emotional exercises?" I ask.

"I put myself in situations and just let the feelings play out. It's a good indicator of how real world situations would play out for me, what I'd feel and what I'd do as a result."

"Tell me more," I say.

"You think it has to do with Quantum Aerobics?"

"Who knows? Just tell me more."

"Last night," he says, "I imagined I was a father, raising a kid from zero, and I realized that what I'd do is psychological abuse. Whenever the kid showed signs of becoming independent I'd squash him. I'd keep him locked up in a mental prison of my making."

I'm thinking: it's probably too late to mess up Tex, but what if it isn't? Somebody should warn him. Let's see what I can do with Ed here.

"What are you guys up to?" asks Lester, coming into the room suddenly. Ed shoots him a rageful look.

"Ed was telling me—"

"Hey, that was between us," says Ed.

"Oh, come on," I say. "Lester's a much better human being than I am. If you were gonna trust me with it, you sure as hell can trust him."

"I don't know," says Ed. "Though I don't mean to suggest—"

"Don't worry," says Lester. "He's just messing with your mind."

"But go ahead," I say. "You were explaining what a sadistic father you'd be. I think Lester would like to hear."

"You were saying you'd be a sadistic father?" asks Lester.

"Oh sweet Jesus," says Ed, turning to me. "Why are you doing this?"

"Because I can," I say.

"What I've found," says Lester "is that if you have such fantasies, it's really saying what was done to you."

"What fantasies?" I ask him.

"You know, squashing independence—"

"So you heard what I was saying," says Ed.

"Only a little."

"Oh sweet Jesus," says Ed.

Just then Tex walks in, and Ed's face registers a sense of deeper betrayal. I actually feel a little for him, but a guy's gotta be able to handle himself in such situations or he's not a guy, right?

Tex gets one whiff of Ed, something happens in his eyes, there's goodness in this kid.

"Look," he says, "other than my Dad, nobody's here to hurt you."

"He's right," I say.

"Professor Blumenthal," says Tex, "there's something I've wanted to ask you."

"What?"

"Let's go in the other room," says Tex.

"Why?"

"It's personal."

They go into the bedroom and close the door. I eavesdrop as best I can.

"You're looking for something from my Dad," says Tex.

"What the hell are you talking about?" asks Ed.

"It's obvious," says Tex. "Let truth rise between us, bathe in a sea of truth."

"Are you in a cult?"

"Just feel it," says Tex. "Just feel this wave of truth sweeping over you. Let yourself know what you already know."

"What exactly are we walking about here?" asks Ed, quiver in his voice, dragged down the rabbit hole.

"You want my Dad to be your father, and I've shown up, and I'm the competition. Am I right?"

"I don't—"

"Sea of truth," says Tex. "Am I right?"

"No," says Ed. "No way. Where the hell do you get off—"

"Sea of truth," says Tex. "Let it go. Let the fear go. Everybody knows it anyway. Just admit it, let the waves wash the pain away in the great sea of truth."

Must be something from his mom, I think. Feels familiar. I do remember the week we spent together: she was 100 percent USDA prime hippie.

The thing that's surprising me is that Ed's getting drawn in, he's relaxing. Wouldn't be if he knew I could hear him. The kid's got something.

"Even if it was a little true—and I suppose we're all looking for parents in some form—"

"It's a pretty widespread need," says Tex, "all the things we didn't get. You and I are allies, we're on the same quest. Really, we are."

"You're saying that I'm looking for my father in that clown."

I have to restrain myself from objecting to the whole clown characterization.

"That's what I'm saying. But you're lucky, because he isn't actually your father. You can look for your father in less toxic places. Me, I'm pretty much stuck."

"Because your Dad really is here."

"That's the deck of cards I've been dealt," says Tex. "Dipped in shit."

"I heard that," I say, can't resist anymore.

"You were listening in?" asks Ed.

"He won't tell anyone," says Tex.

"Why won't I?"

"Because if you do, I'll never have anything to do with you again."

"You're the one who's camped out here," I say. "I never invited you."

"That's how it started, yeah," says Tex. "But we're in act two now. So get away from the damned door, and let us finish our conversation in peace."

A student, God help him, comes to me for assistance.

"What's wrong?" I ask.

"I overheard a conversation among very smart schizophrenics," he says. "They were naming their favorite authors, and it's the same list as mine."

"So you think you're schizophrenic?"

"I'm not saying that," he says.

"I think that's exactly what you're saying."

He storms out of my office. I'm hungry.

"Where did you get to be so smart?" I ask Tex.

"My Dad's Einstein," he says.

"Yeah, there's that I suppose," I say. "But this is emotional knowledge, it's different. Where did you get this from?"

"The quest for father can be a real learning experience," says Tex.

"Are you looking for a hero?" I ask.

"Hey, I already know you better than that."

"Good," I say. "Because society has made it almost impossible, or at least almost too undesirable to be a hero. And it's a shame, because now we have no one through whom to experience the great myths vicariously."

"So we've got to live our lives ourselves."

"Nah, that's too much of a bother."

I glance at the campus newspaper, buzz about a writing prize of ten thousand dollars to be awarded for the finest essay on the topic: The best way to understand the universe is...

Lester and I decide to hike in the nearby woods. Actually, Lester decides, and I'm so weak now I go along.

"So what's really going on with you?" asks Lester.

"I don't really know who I am right now."

"Seriously?"

"Yes."

"Good for you," says Lester.

I dream I'm calling an Intergalactic Police Force, my civic duty, asking them to look into these saboteurs at the center of the universe. Like all good police, at least in movies, they're eating doughnuts. They take my phone number and a family history that runs oh nine hundred pages, stuff even I didn't know, where did you guys get it from? They show me the pages: hieroglyphics.

"I'd like to request a dictionary," I say.

One of the guys laughs.

"How about a Rosetta Stone?"

The guy reaches into a satchel and extracts tablets, three languages side by side. The first is my dream language though not only mine, the second's DNA, and the third looks like Maxwell's equations but the symbols are three-dimensional. I faint and that fainting is waking up.

"Tex, we need to talk," I say.

"Shoot."

"Look," I say. "There's been a definite shift in the power around here, moving toward you and I can't have it."

"I need you, and you need me," says Tex, and he seems to think that's responding to what I said. "I actually know that you're not entirely the jerk you pretend to be, the genome didn't malfunction quite that badly."

"I'd have called you a liar before my breakdown," I say.

"That's the point," says Tex. "We have to work out an arrangement where we don't blackmail each other. Why not just take in the experience, see what we get?"

"Bathe in the ocean of truth."

"You can't mess with people like that," he says. "In my presence, I don't ever want to see you attempting to destroy someone else's mind. Just do it when I'm not around, OK?"

"Why do you care?"

"It offends my sense of decency," says Tex.

"I won't be declawed," I say.

"Just in my presence. And by the way, retinitis pigmentosa's the

Alan Salant *Ablong*

latest."

"What are you talking about?"

"Latest conquest of Quantum Aerobics."

"Really?"

"Yeah. Go figure. Asshole does good despite himself, again."

"What did you tell Ed?" I ask.

"That's between him and me."

"No, I mean about the abusing part."

"Ever hear of Lloyd deMause?"

"Didn't he score the winning touchdown in Super Bowl XIII?"

"He has this theory," says Tex, "about how a baby can become a poison-container. How parents with unresolved pain inject it into the child."

"I just read in *Time Magazine* how moms are now given a syringe on discharge from the maternity ward," I say, contributing to the conversation.

"Cool it, Pops," says Tex.

"I and the public know, what all schoolchildren learn—"

Throw some Auden at the wall, see if it sticks.

"The point is," says Tex, "that the parent now expects—unconsciously, of course—that the baby will give love, that the baby will cleanse the parent's feelings of depression and fear and anger. So the baby, in effect, is now cast in the role of the parent. And if baby cries, then baby isn't being loving."

"And parent goes: whack."

"Right," says Tex.

"And you told Ed that."

"Yep."

"Terrible when a child has to become the parent," I say.

Tex looks at me oddly.

A warm day. Spring's counter-attacked and driven winter way north. The flowers aren't sure what to do but the kids know, they're getting sexual all over campus. The head of Linguistics is peeing in the bushes.

"Shame about Werner," says Tex. Werner's the new breakdown case, now I'm old news. A flurry of departmental politics so upset him that he's slipped into a dream state in which he's speaking a mix of thirty-one languages. Medical opinion is that he'll recover within a year or two, and in the meantime urine's not hurting the plants, just adds spice to the local ecology.

Of course a few hot-headed parents are starting to complain, what are you guys running here, but fortunately our big rival school just had a sex scandal so good that even prostitutes are taking notes, and anyway money's flooding in, prestige has never been higher, and don't even ask about the football team. OK, you asked. They went undefeated.

"He names the plants he pees on," I say. "Names them in all thirty-one languages, including that African clicking language. And most surprising, he names them in Indo-European. Not even his closest friends knew that he speaks conversational Indo-European."

"I'm taking off for a few days, going to Sedona," says Tex. So that's what the packed suitcase is about.

"What's in Sedona?"

"Mom."

"Figures," I say.

"She's happy there," he says. "And it's o so beautiful."

"All that spiritual energy. Do they bill by the kilowatt?"

"Should be back in a week," says Tex, and the truth is, I'm glad he told me.

Faculty dinner, heated argument about whether humanity's improving and my goodness, Ed's involved, not his style. Let's see if I can help.

"Have you read Ed's piece in Vanity Fair?" I ask.

"Not now," says Ed, face flushed.

I get the vibe, take his cue.

"It's unusual," I say. "An academic paper printed directly in a mainstream magazine. It's called *All Alone: Our Universal Orphanhood and the Literary/Political Experience*."

"Vanity Fair?"

"Yes," I say. "Ed argues that the loss of God as parent has cast humanity into despair, we're all orphans now."

"Religious identification is at an astonishingly high level around the world," objects the chairman of Religion.

"Yes," I say, "but Ed looks beneath the surface to construct a new model of the human being, a sequel to Economic Man called Terrified Man. He asks what would happen if a large segment of humanity was actually in denial about its own religious doubts."

"You're saying God doesn't exist?"

"Not me, Ed," I say. "And he's not denying God's existence, it's just a thought experiment asking what the world would look like if most of us had a subconscious suspicion—and since it's subconscious the faculties of the conscious mind couldn't weigh in—that we might

Alan Salant *Ablong*

be alone in the universe."

"Hmm," says our Jungian.

"And using the most current modeling techniques," I continue, "including a breathtaking application of Monte Carlo methods, Ed derives a political, economic, and social realm that looks suspiciously like the one we're in. Ed successfully predicted fluctuations in attitudes on five major issues in the developed world over the past year."

Ed gets up and walks out of the room.

"I read today that your Quantum Aerobics has led to a cure for epilepsy," says a young professor, blonde and hot. She dips her voice in a touch of flirtation and holds her cocktail glass perfectly. She really doesn't understand.

"I didn't see that," I say.

"It's remarkable that you're so blasé about your achievements," she says.

"I can't do anything to stop them," I say.

"Why would you want to stop them?"

"I'm like a novelist whose book becomes a blockbuster movie completely unrelated to his intention."

"How are you like that?"

"I need air," I say, and I go out looking for Ed.

I mention Terrified Man in my next lecture on Quantum Aerobics, and the following day I receive this letter:

Dear Professor Ablong,

You're ignorant about religion. Please stop misleading students about our field.

Sincerely,

The Entire Religion Department

It's a form letter, drawn up for use by a variety of departments. But personalized for me, which is nice.

I toss the letter and realize in that instant that I have the desire to go all Kerouac, just ride the trains, slice across all the categories of the country. I could do it in the summer. But I'm also scared, want to stay close to home, curl up in a ball.

When Tex returns he's all tanned and his rugged good looks are ruggedder and gooder. Tex is a real good-looking kid, his mother was a looker. He's got the aw-shucks innocence, plus the biceps of a lumberjack. And all that psychological knowledge he's gathered tells me that he must really hate himself, otherwise why bother?

Still, I'm surprised to see sadness in his eyes—surprised it's there, and surprised I notice.

"Something happened," I say. "What's wrong, kid?"

"Mom's got cancer," he says. "She's coming east, going to Sloan Kettering for treatment. She doesn't want to leave Sedona, believe me."

"You knew she was sick?"

"I knew something was wrong," he says. "Just from her voice."

"You're really a good guy," I say. "How did that happen?"

"Now you know why I need you," he says.

"I don't say this often," I say, "but that one actually went over my head."

"I feel too much," says Tex. "I need more of an asshole side."

"Then you came to the right place," I say.

"I'm not so sure," he says. "You're threatening to go soft. I should have come sooner."

"Let me understand this," I say. "You're telling me—"

"I don't know if it's those mirror cells science is talking about, how we feel what's in the other guy. But I just have too much of it."

OK, that gets me thinking.

When I hit it big with my theory, when I did enough for a lifetime in one bowel movement, I got to step outside the programming for a minute, felt I'd justified my existence, and until that moment I never knew that I felt a need to justify my existence. That's why I could just ride the trains, or imagine doing it, because this society doesn't have anything to shame me with, except my dreams.

Tex has gotten a bad habit lately of singing softly, almost under his breath, the stream of his own consciousness.

"You really wanted to sleep with your mother?" I ask.

"Why do you say that?"

"Because you talk to yourself," I say. "And that's what just came out."

"I know I talk to myself," he says. "And I know exactly what I say when I talk to myself. And that's not what I said."

It was worth a try.

Lester's been bedridden with mono, now he's back. These days I can't seem to keep anyone out of my living-room. He and Tex are talking. It's like Tex invoked him, needs him. This need thing, damn. Give me John Wayne, don't need nobody, who cares that he didn't serve during the war, is it the sperm counts, down sixty percent since 1955? And naturally we invent nice theories, how we're getting in touch with our feelings. Reason's the eye of the storm.

I complain about it to Tex, part of parenting.

"What's the difference," he asks, "between spending your life needing people, and spending your life not needing people? Either way, you die."

"Yeah, but one way's moral and manly," I say. "The other way's weak and flabby. And you kind of dissolve."

"I'll keep it in mind," says Tex, walks out the door.

"So what did you do while you were sick, Lester?"

"Watched a lot of TV."

"And what did you see?"

"The dreamlife of this society is really messed up," says Lester. "Bring in that shit to a shrink, and he'll have the lot of us committed."

"What do you mean?"

"I think one out of every three series is about serial killers," he says. "And the rest is the reality shows."

"Oh, everybody hates those," I say. "They're only on because of the ratings."

Lester coughs.

"Hey, cover your mouth," I say. "We don't know what you're spreading. And anyway, monsters are good for us. They let us practice coping with reality."

That's a mistake, leads to a long conversation, and eventually Tex returns. It's a hot day, summer preview. He jumps in the shower to dry himself off with water.

"How's your mom?" asks Lester when Tex emerges from the bathroom.

"So far so good," he says. Yeah, I suppose I could've asked.

Lester's excited because while he was sick he got word that he'd been granted a fellowship to go to some coral reef somewhere in a year or two.

"Not seeing how that's gonna advance your legal career," I tell him.

"You know," says Lester, "insisting that I'm pre-law isn't going to make it happen."

"The world's what we believe it is," I say. "And coral reefs are a bad bet these days. They're all dying."

"I'm going to try and help save them." says Lester.

"I'm just not sure that they respond to legal arguments," I say.

Lester and Tex exchange a glance that tells me the power is shifting further against me in my own home and that a few weeks apart hasn't put distance between them.

There was one day in my life, fortunately only one, when I imagined everyone else in the world was connected except me. People were all soul-mates, they were all in tune, except me. I'm remembering it now, and with it come other memories that got grouped with it in my brain according to the bizarre filing system of the drunk librarian who runs the place. Something about peanut butter.

"So what exactly is Quantum Aerobics?" asks Tex.

"You have Wikipedia," I say. "I got it for you for your birthday."

"I mean it," he says.

"Ah hell," I say. "Step one, musical patterns are converted into roller-coaster rides that turn out to provide unprecedented thrills. Next, an analysis of the digestive system produces new and even better roller-coaster rides. Those curves, the curves of the roller-coaster track, turn out to explain aspects of ecology. Rhythms of *Finnegans Wake* are found to match the textures and flows of the body of math. Got it?"

"That's the exact explanation you gave me last night in a dream," he says.

"You're learning," I say.

"You think I'm kidding," he says.

That shakes me up a bit. What if reality has fracture lines like a rock, and sometimes it just plain comes apart, and we're left without causality, statistical law collapses, actuarial tables go bad?

"All right," I say. "You know how before Galileo's time the heavens were seen as different from earth."

"No," he says.

"Did you attend school?"

"I was absent that day," he says.

"The day they taught about the rise of modern science?"

"No, the day they held school."

OK, that would be a different society.

"The heavens," I say. "Heaven was supposed to be made of a special substance, the quintessence, the fifth element. Heaven and earth were seen as having different principles. Things in heaven moved naturally in circles, while on earth things moved in straight lines."

"OK."

"But the point is that math is traditionally seen as being distinct from reality. Quantum Aerobics shows that math and reality operate by the same principles."

"No shit? Are you serious?"

"When you put it that way, I'm not entirely sure," I say.

"No," he says. "I'm really curious. Is that what it's about?"

"Do you care?"

"I've been asking around. And that's the first explanation that fits at all."

"In what way?"

"I mean, I can see what the fuss is about."

"There's more," I say. "Theater's a condensation of life. But life, it turns out, is a condensation of something else." And these green guys, I think, are a condensation of theater. An image half-forms in my mind.

Tex brings by a new friend of his, guy named George Rhyth.

"Spell that."

He does.

"Do you realize you're just one letter short of all the good stuff?" I ask.

"I think you guys might enjoy talking," says Tex, and he goes out on the porch. We stare at each other.

"I don't really understand my son's thought process," I say.

Rhyth begins looking down, can't quite meet my glance. I can torture this guy.

"Hmm," he says.

He's still checking out his shoes. I begin to worry what's inside them, and what would happen if it got out.

He reiterates. "Hmm."

In a sudden wave of illumination I understand his predicament. He's been told what a bastard I am, and he's shy about confessing it because he doesn't want to hurt my feelings.

"Look," I say. "If you're worried that you'll say something to me that no one else has, I can put your mind entirely at ease."

He lifts his head slowly and looks at me with wide astonished eyes.

"How did you know what I was thinking?"

"I think you've been briefed," I say.

"Briefed about what?"

"How well do you know my son?"

"I'm not sure what scale to use in measuring that," he says.

"I'm gonna go watch some TV," I say, and I go into the bedroom and close the door.

"George wasn't happy when he left," says Tex later that night.

"I hope I didn't have anything to do with that," I say.

"You had everything to do with it," says Tex. "You rudely went into the other room and closed the door."

"I went into the other room," I said. "But I didn't realize I did it rudely. Was it the way I walked?"

"The rudeness was—oh, hell. You might really have enjoyed talking to this guy."

"Why?

"Because you might have."

"I might have enjoyed talking to a green ball of ooze," I say. "It doesn't mean I'll do it. But why do people keep coming by?"

"What do you mean?"

"There are much nicer people in the world to visit."

"They feel comfortable here," says Tex.

"But why?"

"It's your personality," says Lester, from the kitchen. I didn't even know he was there. "You're everyone's first experience of the world, where it looks like all it does is bite."

A week later: Rhyth is back.

"I want you to see this," he says.

He puts in a DVD which, he explains, was filmed on a recent date.

"You could have just said it was filmed recently."

"No, I wanted to make the point that it was filmed on a date."

"Everything happens on a date," I say. "It's part of the space-time grid. Get used to it. And wash behind your ears."

"I don't mean a date in time," he says.

"Well, what other kind is there?" Maybe the green fellows could help out on this.

"I mean, two people out on a date."

My mind is taking it in literally so I have an image of them walking along the surface of a calendar. I look at him helplessly.

"A date," he repeats. "Two people. Wine, roses..."

"Oh, you mean a date." Wait for it, thoughts realign. "You filmed your date?"

"Yes."

"Why?"

"I wanted to see if what happened was what I thought had happened."

"Did she know you were filming it?"

"Yes."

"And she didn't object?"

"It was her idea."

"It can't have been a very spontaneous experience," I say.

"It was," he said. "Hyper-spontaneous. At first, yes, we were self-conscious, but then we forgot, and it was as if the parts of our brain that normally held back—the designated watcher, if you would—realized they could join in, so we were entirely in the experience."

"That's not what would happen to me if I was taping."

"Just watch, OK?"

"Is there sex?"

"No," he says.

"See, that's the effect of taping it."

"Just watch," he says.

"You're sure there's no sex?"

"Yes."

"It so happens," I say, "that I have the third largest porn collection on the Eastern seaboard."

"I didn't actually know that," says Rhyth, thinks a minute. "How do you know? How is that measured?"

"By reputation," I say.

"That can't be the right metric," he says.

"OK then: by temperature," I say.

"Just watch the damn DVD," he says.

It's a breathtaking place, somewhere out West judging by the red rocks. He's with this woman, red hair and musical curves, I'm sure a lot of guys would like to play that instrument. They're sitting high above a valley, lushness of red.

"Now it all fits," I say. "I can see why you filmed a date with her."

"It was her idea," he repeats. "Now will you watch?"

"Your wish is my demand," I say.

"Command," he says.

"Let the waters part," I say.

"Sorry?"

"You told me to command, so I did."

He thinks. "Oh, so you're God now."

"I've always wanted to play God," I say. "Maybe in a short-length film—"

My attention's caught by the expression on the woman's face, the most beautiful look I've ever seen.

"Her name's Beatrice, right?" I ask.

"How did you know that?"

"You're kidding, right?"

"Tex must have told you."

"No," I say. "I don't know if you're kidding or not."

"I'm not. But how did you know?"

"It's how I've always imagined Dante's Beatrice would look," I say.

"Well then, wait for this," he says.

"Look, Rhyth," she says. "Why not make the goal of your writing to be as creative as possible, and as thorough over the surface of your entire life as possible?"

"She's talking to you about writing?"

"Yes."

An involuntary shiver passes over my body, this is one of those moments where you just wonder. As if there's a wave of synchronicity and meaning that just sweeps over the globe like one of those pinging things on an air-traffic controller's grid except in three dimensions, maybe more. Sweeps over it and lands at particular places, and for all I know it's subject to Newton's laws of motion.

Inside my head the little green guys are talking, first time ever without broccoli. No turning back now.

"So what happens next?" I ask.

"Why are you asking?" he asks. "Just let the movie unfold."

The beauty of the scene's overwhelming me. A rich sun pours its light over the entire valley and I feel as if I can see every shadow.

"Supposedly in his later years Newton could tell time by the shadows of buildings," I say.

"You're spoiling the moment," he says.

He's right.

"I'd like to be as thorough over her surface as possible," I say.

He turns red-faced toward me and then he chuckles.

"Swear to God," he says. "I had exactly the same thought."

OK, they didn't do it or he wouldn't have said that, wasted date, nothing to see here. And yet the way he's looking at her, I realize I'm watching a magical moment in his life and I actually feel shame, a sense of violating him. His fault.

"Why did you want me to see this?"

"I want witness to the moment," he says.

"But you witnessed it, and she did too."

Now he clams up, has me wondering, a signal for the full paranoia of my mind to come out and play.

After dinner.

"You've got it all," says Tex.

"I know I'm loaded," I say.

"It's not the money I'm talking about," says Tex. "How many people have so many folks so filled with gratitude toward them? The whole world is ready to love you. Just let them."

"That would be too easy," I say.

"What does that even mean?"

"I don't know," I say.

"You probably don't," says Tex. "And that's a big problem."

"And you have the solution."

"No," he says. "All I can offer is to identify it as a problem."

"Why do you care so much about me?"

"It's like in *Back to the Future*," says Tex. "I need a happy father to be a fulfilled son."

"So it's all about you."

"Of course it's all about me."

"Really?" I ask, and I'm sad. "You don't know how to get beyond yourself either?"

A worldwide conspiracy claims another victim: I enter therapy.

The couch isn't that comfortable. I point out that with eighty million dollars in the bank I could buy her a better couch.

"I don't know if that's a good idea," Jume says. Had to ask three times to get the right spelling, and she was perplexed when I kept sticking in a silent h.

"Why not?" I ask about the couch idea.

"That might involve crossing a boundary."

"I don't mean it sexually," I say.

"I find it interesting," she says, "that you bring up sex."

"Let me clarify something," I say. "Do I have to be concerned about your feelings? Because if so, this is probably a bad idea."

"No," she says. "I'll take care of my feelings, we're here to work on yours."

"Well then," I say. "I've slept with enough women—"

"Eight thousand, I've heard."

"It's confidential in here, right?"

"Yes."

"That number isn't accurate," I say.

A month into therapy I suddenly blurt out about the broccoli creatures.

"So what do you think?" I ask.

"Well," she says, "I have to begin from the obvious fact that you're an asshole. So this is probably a big put-on."

"I thought you're trained to know what's real and what isn't."

"Yes," she says. "But you're different."

It's my last chance to turn back.

"I'm not making it up," I say. "Do a Vulcan mind-meld or give me some sodium pentothal. I heard it comes in cherry."

Jume uncrosses and re-crosses her legs.

"Look," I say. "I know this is the price I pay for being me. But I'm not making it up about the broccolites."

"All right," she says. "I'm giving you the chance to make a complete fool of me, to show that my command of the real world isn't worth a dime. To go to all your colleagues and say you got your therapist to believe you eat broccoli and these beings near the center of the universe—"

"It's the truth," I say.

"Fine," she says. "Why do you think it's happening to you?"

"I don't know. And I don't know why I was born either. Lately it seems there's a lot I don't know. You wake up in this mystery, and you go to school, and you make money, and the basic question's never answered: why are we let in through this door?"

"I want to talk to you at this level," she says, leaning forward. "I just don't trust you enough to do it."

"And whose fault is that?"

"You've spent a month throwing every kind of bullshit at me that you can think up. So I'd say it's your fault."

"I should explain," I say, "that since early childhood I've operated on the principle that nothing's ever my fault."

"Why do you think that is?" she asks.

What's with all the questions?

Tex is smoking a joint when I come home.

"That'll stunt your growth," I say.

"I don't think marijuana does that," he says. "And it's a bit late, anyway. How was your day?"

I tell him about my session.

"I think you need a new therapist," he says.

"Why?"

"Because this one understands you too well."

"Any comments about the broccoli?" I ask.

"Groovy," he says, and drops off to sleep.

I tell Jume that Tex thinks I need a new therapist.

"Because?"

"Because you know me too well."

She smiles. "So I take it you're staying with me."

"How did you know?"

"Tell me more about the broccolites."

"I'm feeling an entirely new kind of helplessness," I say. "Like I'm flying through the air and I don't know who propelled me up, and I can't change course."

"So you're a missile."

"And I'm wondering if there's something I'm supposed to be doing, and maybe the answer's in the air, but the air's a bit tight-lipped, need-to-know-basis and all that."

"How long have you felt that way?" asks Jume.

"Did you get those diplomas on the Internet?" I ask.

She looks at them for a moment. "No. How long?"

"It's been coming for a few months," I say.

"And why do you think it's happening to you?"

"Maybe I just cut loose too much from everything. Maybe my fame and money have cut me free of all demands."

"You sound scared," she says.

"I think the whole point of human drama is to keep us from thinking about this stuff," I say.

"What sort of drama?"

"The wars, the rich and powerful abusing the poor and weak, the persistence of in-laws. And I've stepped out of it, and it's no good. I just can't stop my brain from asking these questions."

"And what are you most afraid of?"

"Hell," I say. "Unlimited pain and punishment."

"And this is a new fear for you?"

"It's getting scarier by the day. I hope you can help me."

"Start meditating," she says. "It shrinks the fear center and increases one's sense of calm."

"If I make it home," I say.

"You can do it in the garden," she says, pointing. "It's a beautiful day. Or you can sit in my waiting room after the session if you want."

Somehow that feels good. I'm clutching my lifeboat, Earth, this existence, hoping that in the green fields, the breath of her vast skies, she has something for me.

The broccolites have a giant circulatory system running through what functions as their cities, and it sends thoughts and feelings around. It's run by a utility similar to Con Edison. No, that's my waking vision, it distorts.

It's happened a half dozen times by now. I have to sit quietly to remember what I saw. The circulatory bit's what my waking mind makes of the reality, finds a comfortable category.

"Go dark," says Jume.

"What do you mean by that?"

"What's the worst situation you can imagine?" she asks.

"Needing someone," I say, just comes out of my mouth.

"That's interesting," she says.

"If the universe is made entirely of water," I say, "the way Thales thought—" And I stop. I know it annoys her.

"Yes?"

"Sorry?"

"Tick tock," she says. "Moment by moment you and I are dying. Do you really want to waste our time?"

"Yes, actually."

She picks up her copy of *The Palm at the End of the Mind*, it's always beside her, and starts reading.

"All right," I say after a few minutes.

"For real?"

"What I was saying was that if the universe is made entirely of water—and by water I assume he means a general fluid like the ether of the 19th century, though he's unavailable for questioning—then we're water."

"So?"

"I—"

She's interested now.

"Come out with it," she says.

"I have wished deeply for an interconnection with all things," I say.

"And?"

"I really have," I say, surprising myself again. "And—"

"And?"

"I live an inexpressible loneliness and my heart went cold long ago, and I don't know why."

She's listening, sure, but it occurs to me that Jume is flipping out. She's bringing food to sessions, pass the breast-milk.

"Is this standard?" I ask when she hands me a tray of lasagna.

"I'm not traditional," she says.

"But you know what you're doing, right?"

"I'm just following a feeling," she says. "I think this is going to

Alan Salant *Ablong*

open something."

Her lasagna is really good.

"I thought it was reciprocal," says Lester.

He's bummed out because there's a grad student he was crazy about and she just conveyed how deeply she'd love to be friends.

Tex is his usual sympathetic, and I see young Lester's hurting. I do see it, and it occurs to me there's no reason to add to his pain, and there's a high probability that anything I say would add to his pain, so I shut up.

"Life sucks," says Tex.

"Man, I thought it would be easier," says Lester.

Lester was an orphan. He told me when we went walking in the woods. He was raised in an orphanage and his real parent was science. He discovered it as a kid—a smart kid—and all the calm in his life came from science: reading about it, doing the experiments, feeling that the whole scientific world, the whole scientific method, was his home, his family. Any time he'd read about Boyle or Newton he just felt something in the universe was smiling at him, lighting the empty marathon corridors of his psyche, a calm cool cream on all the exposed bruises, the secret aching places in his soul.

I tell Jume about Lester.

"You seem emotional," she says. Today she's baked a moussaka. "Anything in Lester's story that coincides with yours?"

"I was a smart kid too," I say.

"So you've mentioned," she says. "More than once. Anything else?"

"I don't know if this matters," I say.

"Tell me," she says.

"It's probably not important."

"Just say it."

"I'm an orphan too."

That gets her eyebrows up.

"No shit?"

"Is that the latest in psychoanalytic terminology?"

"Are you offended by profanity?" she asks.

"No," I say. "I'm offended by its absence."

She processes.

"Tell me more about being an orphan."

"I was raised in an orphanage too," I explain. "Nobody came to claim me. Nobody wanted me."

She takes out a cigarette, swear to God.

"Mind if I smoke?" she asks.

"Not really," I say. "But can't you be disbarred?"

"That's law."

"Ex-communicated?"

"Catholicism."

"Defrocked, disenfranchised, dishonorably discharged, discorporated, deflowered, annulled, deloused—"

She takes a long deep puff.

"I'm commemorating one of the most surprising moments in my life as a therapist," she says.

"Come on," I say. "You've heard juicier. Love triangle involving Dad and two non-humans, kid chained in the basement and forced to read the unabridged *Kapital*—"

"It isn't the way you make it sound," says Jume, exhaling a big smoke ring.

"How do I make it sound?"

"Like nobody wanted you."

"That's because nobody wanted me."

"Yes, but that was a very particular situation," she says. "Very few people knew you were out there to want."

In my mid-forties I tried to trace my origins but the search led to a dead end.

"I really don't know how to live," I say. "I feel like I'm making my life up out of little segments of what other people do."

"Measuring out your life in coffee-spoons."

"Huh?" I know Prufrock, but heck, make her earn her pay.

"It's from a poem," she says.

"Don't put words in my mouth," I say. "And especially not poems."

"Sorry," she says. "But seriously, you don't like poems?"

"Poetry is the last refuge of the incompetent."

"I think that quote goes differently."

"I'm not quoting anyone," I say. "Now you're putting my words in someone else's mouth. You really should look into that."

"You're being you," she says. "Stop it."

"How anti-therapist of you."

"I know," she says. "I can't believe I just said it. Kind of glad, though."

"Look," I say. "I'm not kidding. I feel like somebody should be telling me what to do, and nobody is, and it's like all the gravity of earth has been turned off, not a single atom on the planet cares to pull me in, and I'm just out there floating away."

Alan Salant *Ablong*

"It's called freedom," she says. "And it can be terrifying."

"Wait a minute," I say. "This is a good thing?"

"It's the work of centuries, millennia," she says. "One person at a time. You're feeling it now."

"My guess is the old hunter-gatherers felt freer than we ever will," I say.

Evening wraps late afternoon in its arms, squeezes out the last rays, wrings the day-rag dark.

"I don't know if I'm going crazy," I tell Tex. By now the line between therapy and non-therapy's blurring, I'm just telling everybody everything.

"With you," he asks, "how could one tell?"

"I'm serious," I say.

"So am I," he says.

"No," I say, "I'm really serious."

"So am I," he says.

"I'm scared," I say. "I need you to tell me if I'm sane or not."

"I don't know enough about sanity to say," says Tex. "What does the shrink say?"

"She says I'm looking at freedom and it's terrifying me."

"Is she right?"

"That's what I don't know."

"When I get agitated," says Tex, "I sometimes sit just imagining what's going on everywhere in the world. Sometimes if I can't sleep I do it too. What's happening right now in Mumbai, on the Serengeti, three feet underwater in the mid-Atlantic, in a volcanic crater with those strange heat-loving bacteria."

"If I did that," I say, "I'd get indigestion."

"Why?"

"I have a bad digestive system," I say.

"No," says Tex. "I mean, why would you get indigestion from imagining?"

"I thought I explained that," I say. "I have a bad digestive system. By the way, how's your time machine coming?"

"I'm not working on a time machine," says Tex.

"Maybe it's Ed who's working on it," I say.

At the next faculty meeting I announce that Ed's been working on a time machine.

"Really?" asks a new hire. "What sort of progress have you been making, Ed?"

"I'm not working on a time machine," says Ed.

"He's too modest," I say. "Of course, maybe this is just future Ed. Possibly future Ed: are you from the future?"

"I'm the same Ed I've always been," he says.

"I'll double-check with the secretary in Psychology," I say, "but I think the current paradigm opposes personal stasis. But as a novelist you'd know better than I."

I turn to the professor next to me.

"The thing to understand about Ed's fiction," I explain, "is that he's a believer in the return to water, that coming out of the ocean was a mistake, and he's showing us the way back. An underwater culture, dolphin civilization. His writing is water, fluid, it bypasses the solid land of a novel, makes you put aside your assumptions. It's the Einstein feeling, let go the familiar. Isn't that right, Ed?"

"You're absolutely right," says Ed.

Ah, I think, trying a new tack, vanishing.

That night under broccoli I imagine Ed's gone, replaced by a vast novel in wisps of cloud. Random at first, but after three or four thousand pages a pattern appears, by page nine thousand it's showing all my denied feelings, denied perspectives, the life I've never lived, the openness of the universe, world where need isn't evil. The fantasy makes me hungry, I order an entire pizza. Its arrival is Lester's cue to emerge from the guest room, no idea he was there. I'm glad: my eyes were bigger than my stomach.

A very serious news show, something British, is reporting on the dance of a tribe found in the last remote place on earth. Carbon dating establishes that the dance was created in pre-Copernican times. Nine people are circling around one, and some are circling around some of those. There's film from above, yes, you'd think you were looking at the solar system.

"Amazing," says Tex.

"Not really," I say. "Remember, there are only eight planets now that Pluto's been sent down to the minors. And Jupiter doesn't have nearly enough moons. And where are the comets, and the Oort cloud?"

"You're taking it too literally," says Lester, who apparently was eating again in the kitchen. "So what if they missed a few moons here and there. How did they know what they knew?"

"It could be coincidence," I say.

"Or maybe they were visited by aliens," suggests Lester.

"Or they had primal visions," says Tex.

Alan Salant *Ablong*

"I thoroughly believe that you need a telescope to see Saturn's moons," I say. "And these guys don't sound like they had one back then."

"Maybe they were visited by a time traveler," says Tex.

"I think the rule is," I say, "that a time machine can't go back to a time before the machine was created."

"Who made that rule?" asks Lester.

"I heard it somewhere," I say.

"Then we need to get cracking on making a time machine," says Tex, "or we'll be missing out on a whole lot of stuff." And he and Lester go into the other room.

I may not be right, but it seems that Lester is now living in my house. That I didn't invite him seems less and less relevant. Lester sleeps on a fold-out cot.

Rhyth's also around, but I don't think he's living here.

"It's when I wrapped up her clothes that it really hit me," Rhyth says. "That's when I really knew she's gone."

He's talking about his mother. She died last year. I have this image of a different kind of anatomy, a book that just tells these kinds of things. Page four: when you wrap up the clothes of a dead beloved, that's when you know she's gone. The emotional bone structure.

Tex walks in, he was out shopping. His hair looks different.

"What the fuck?" I ask, pointing.

"I'm going post-industrial," he says.

He's legally changed his name to Tex, despite warnings from a lot of people that this might lead to the dissolution of his identity. He says he's doing it because he wants to get closer to me.

"But when you become who someone else wants you to be—"

"I'm not becoming that person," he says. "Don't confuse the menu with the meal. I'm still the same guy, just under a different name."

Tex lives as Tex for about three months, and then decides he's gotten what he needed, changes his name back to whatever it was.

Lester's stoned, and so's Tex, and they're trying to make sense of a legal document. It takes me a few minutes to realize it's about renting an apartment. I could help. Nah.

"Under penalty of deforestation," says Tex, squinting at the fine print. "Yeah, that's what it seems to be saying."

"That's heavy, man," says Lester.

"I wouldn't sign," says Tex. "Not with that clause."

"Well wait," says Lester. "We should see what else there is, maybe it gets better."

"Shall in no way be limited," reads Tex.

"See, it's improving already," says Lester. "Universal consciousness baby, no limits."

"Nah, that's just boilerplate," says Tex.

"Let me take a look," says Lester, turning it upside-down. "See, here's your problem. It's in Etruscan."

Tex begins fumbling through papers, all kinds of objects.

"Whatcha lookin' for, man?" asks Lester

"I think my old man has an English-Etruscan dictionary."

"That wouldn't help," says Lester.

"Why not?"

"We need one that goes the other way."

"Right," say Tex after a pause. "Right. It has to go Etruscan-English. I don't think I've seen that one."

"I don't know that I'm gonna sign," says Lester, taking another puff.

"Yeah, we better get a doctor to look it over."

"Know why Judaism's the only religion of the ancient Near East that made it to the modern world?" asks Lester.

"No, do you?"

"No," says Lester. "Wait, because they wrote it down. It's all in the technology. By the way"—he's addressing me now, or whatever version of me appears in his marijuana fog—"what kind of name's Ablong?"

"It's Amorite."

"Like Biblical?"

"Yep."

"You mean you can trace your ancestry—"

"All the way back, baby."

"So what, you worship Baal, vegetative fertility rituals, you do sacrifices?"

"Nah," I say. "We're Reform."

Rhyth keeps almost getting it, applying his energy to a particular task, several times he's almost set up in a stable career but then the sheer vastness of the universe distracts him, he calls it the joy-joy-joy, the triple joy of experiencing its infinite complexity and variety, just feeling it, he's non-sexual during these periods and this becomes his orgasm. Whenever he says triple joy it makes me think Chinese so I always order a delivery of moo shu.

"I worry about Rhyth," says Tex.

Cases like this aren't unusual where hallucinogens are involved, but this guy's clean. He just sees something...

"Is he happy?"

Tex scratches his thin beard. "He seems to be."

"Then what are you worried about?"

"Maybe you're right," says Tex.

But I'm not sure. Is it this sense that we're three-dimensional on a curved four-dimensional surface which is entirely moral, and everything we do is being watched by a judging God who's right next to us always, but because we're dimensionally challenged we don't see Him? And that we're going to be held to account? Naked before God I imagine myself so helpless that it needs a new word. Is that what's worrying Tex?

"Or I might be wrong," I say.

"I'm worried," he says, "that somewhere down the road Rhyth's gonna open a statement of his bank account and find a cold zero staring at him. And that any woman he loves won't want to go along on that particular ride."

"So he'll get a job."

"Yeah, if he can find someone to pay him for grooving on the universe."

"That's called being an artist," I say. "Or a scientist."

"But you have to follow the rules of the board game," says Tex. "You have to start at the beginning and get your various diplomas."

"Is that what those board games are teaching us?" I ask.

"You're making light of it."

"This problem I can fix," I say. "How much does the guy need for the rest of his life?"

"You're giving away your money?"

"I'm starting to like the idea of sharing," I say.

I look up my entry on Wikipedia on the laptop at my bedside.

"Wilson Ablong was born in 1964," it claims. "He's the founder of Quantum Bio-technics, which has been used to cure dozens of diseases in the past few years. He is currently a Professor at—"

I skim the flatteringly long article, stuff I didn't remember about myself, maybe didn't ever know.

"I told you," says Lila, sharing my bed.

Lila's a spineless liberal. She then relates a story that starts with a group of robber-barons surveying land that would be worth a lot if there wasn't a group of tenements on it.

"Here's what they do," she says. "They put in upscale benches in the crack-ridden playgrounds."

"And?"

Apparently the tenement teenagers, expressing what the adults are too adult to express, understand immediately that something alien's been introduced into their territory, not meant for them, so they deface it.

"Right-wing hate radio has a field day," she says. "About these sub-humans, see how these animals are? How they spit on a good thing, these beautiful benches, reject what's positive in the world. They're not fit for good things. We are."

"You sound angry," I say. "Want some broccoli?"

We're still in bed. I keep a log, started it when I was 17, same age Gauss started his diary of math discoveries, entries like Σ Y R H K A ! Num$= \Delta + \Delta + \Delta$. Mine's less math, although you do find an occasional Eureka here too.

"I know a guy," she says. "He's having an attack of conscience."

"There's over-the-counter stuff he could take," I say.

She rolls toward me.

"Do you ever use that mouth for good instead of evil?"

"You tell me," I say, and a few minutes later she's pretty happy.

"Ben Franklin," she says a few minutes after that, "said that democracy is two wolves and a sheep deciding on lunch. Know what freedom is?"

"Never having to say you're sorry?"

She hits me on the arm.

"Forget it," she says. Thinks a minute. "Know what I'm working on?"

"Don't tell me, let me guess," I say. "An explanation of how when one speaks of unconscious conflicts plaguing us today it's no abstraction, but something that creates seemingly unsolvable problems in our daily lives. Things we think we must have or do, that we wouldn't consider necessary if these conflicts didn't exist."

"That's not it," she says.

"We're not talking merely," I say, "about the West's conflicts with Communism or now Islam, but about things that form compulsions in us so we're less flexible. Scaring us so we act to make things worse. Do you have any idea how much of what we call personality, that we see as purely us, is the imprint of unresolved issues?"

"That really isn't it."

"Are you sure? Because we're mostly passive recipients of our creation. Much of what we fill our lives with is there for the most ancient and arbitrary of reasons, and oy, the trouble it causes."

Alan Salant *Ablong*

"Should I tell you what I'm actually writing about?"

"If you must."

"I'm studying how decisions are made in our society. Like health care: who wins, and who loses. Going back to the year 1800."

"What about health care?"

"Oh, HMOs—"

"Too generous," I say. "Any patient applied for reimbursement to me, I'd turn him down."

"On what grounds?"

"Because he's human, that's a pre-existing condition."

She starts to answer, notices a book on my night-table.

"What are you reading?"

It's in Armenian. I don't read Armenian, but I'm building the legend so I carry the book around with me, dropped it off on the night-table when I got home. Other days I carry Polish.

"It's a philosophic treatise," I say. "Just a little pleasure reading."

"Treatise about what?"

"Oh, this guy thinks we're in a trance when we're young, the trance that lets animals imitate their parents and survive, and society learns to exploit it and the military learns to break us and then use the trance to re-form us."

"Trance?"

"You know, the period when we just take the world in and don't question, don't ask why things are the way they are. The worshipful period."

"OK."

"He asks what would happen if we were socialized not to draw sustenance from owning things, but rather from sharing. If we didn't form attachments to objects. If we didn't feel empty if we had no status."

She's looking increasingly puzzled.

"Can I see that?" she asks.

"Here."

She holds the book up, opens it, flips through a few pages.

"It's a cookbook," she says.

"I suppose technically," I say.

"I'm Armenian," she says. "Want to know the things you can do with lamb?"

This morning Tex woke me at eight.

"Don't you have a lecture?"

I stare at the clock, trying to remember who talked me into this.

"You're right," I say. "Want to give it for me?"

"Not particularly," he says.

"You don't have to talk about Quantum Aerobics. Tell them what it's like to have me as your Dad. They'll probably like it better."

"You want me to go up there and say that you asked me to talk about what it's like to be your son."

"Yes," I say, turning over to go back to sleep.

He does it, the kid has balls.

I wake about a minute later to find that he's pouring water on me. Oh, I dreamt that he gave the lecture.

"Hey," I say.

"Get up," he says.

"You're not supposed to water your old man," I say.

It's dawning on me that this water isn't, well, cold.

"What are you, crazy?" I ask. "You'll burn me."

"Not if you get up."

I grant an interview.

"How did you come to write for *Fisherman's Weekly*?" I ask.

"It's not *Fisherman's Weekly*," he says over the phone. "It's the *Journal of the American Mathematical Association*."

"I could have sworn it was *Fisherman's Weekly*."

"Suppose we start with what you're reading these days."

"A wonderful book," I say. "It examines what's really happening on the first day of third grade. Biologically, historically, what's going on at all levels, a modern *Finnegans Wake*, all human consciousness condensed into a few hundred pages. A kid watching, not pretending to feel what he doesn't."

"Not a math book, I take it."

"I don't know," I say. "It's called *Introduction to Differential Geometry*."

"They said this wouldn't be easy," says the interviewer.

"I gather you drew the short straw," I say. "Relax. Swift's society produced Swift to discuss its horrors, and a few centuries later the deepened totalitarian impulse—"

"This is in response to what question?"

"The one you'd have asked if you'd been born one day later than you were."

The new magnetic parlors just off campus are a hit. Stick your head under a magnet for an hour and your thoughts align. A few side-effects, sure: some guys came out screaming, but that just adds to the cachet.

Alan Salant *Ablong*

"Lester and I are going there, wanna come?" asks Tex.

"No," I say. "I'll watch the effect on you first."

"I think I saw God," says Tex, when they return.

"You think?"

"I didn't quite get there," he says.

"And you Lester?"

His face is pale.

"I saw my birth family," he says. "This time they kept me, they raised me, I felt this peace I've never felt. I've spent my whole life looking for this."

He goes back the next day, the next, the company paid researchers to write that it isn't addictive. If you squeeze lemon juice into your mouth just before going in, you can reduce the habit-forming effect.

Tex is getting worried about Lester, seems he gets worried about everybody, so finally he stages an intervention.

"What the fuck is this?" asks Lester when he walks in.

"We think you need to stop going to the magneto zone," says Tex.

"It's what I've wanted all my life," says Lester.

"But you've stopped living," says Tex.

"No I haven't."

"You've stopped doing coursework, I barely see you."

"Nothing else is as important to me. My answers are there. I'm leaving."

"No," says Tex, suddenly looking very big.

"I'll kill you," says Lester.

"Listen to yourself," says Tex. "You're addicted. You know it. You won't find your family there, it's an illusion."

"Best illusion of my damned life."

"You're a sensible guy, Lester. Most sensible guy I've ever met. You know it isn't real."

Lester lunges at Tex, Tex sidesteps, Lester crashes into the wall barely protecting his head, shoulder takes most of the punishment. He lies motionless.

"Thinks he's dead?" I ask.

"Doubt it," says Tex. "Hey Lester, you dead?"

Lester groans.

"Look what you're doing," says Tex in this voice I'm pretty sure he got from his mom. "See what the magnets are doing to you?"

Lester gets up slowly, holding his head.

"Oh, goddamn," he says, and starts crying, cries and cries.

"So what have we all learned from this experience?" I ask after a few minutes of Lester wailing.

Tex shoots me a look that in some cultures could kill.

"The way you talk about people," I tell Aretha of Semiotics, "is what strikes me."

She's been describing a drama involving her brother's family, explaining each member's motivations in psychoanalytic detail.

"What do you mean?" she asks.

"You speak of the unconscious so easily. You trace people's lives so easily. If it's that easy—"

"Then how come the world isn't better?"

"Exactly," I say.

Since the intervention Lester has a new serenity.

"I still don't get it," I tell Tex. "He's had all the hope ripped out of him. Why's he so calm?"

"You realize Lester's right here," says Tex.

"I know."

Tex looks at Lester.

"Because I've stopped wasting energy on having the family I wish I had, I've realized that my deepest needs won't be met," says Lester. "All that energy freed up for real things. And I've realized that I can live without that imaginary family."

"So?" I ask.

"What do you mean, so?"

"I mean, what does one have to do with the other?"

"What does realizing he can live without that imaginary family have to do with becoming calmer?" asks Tex. "Have you ever had an emotional insight?"

"Not that I know of. Why do you ask?"

"Do you actually not know?"

"In a way, I actually don't know," I say.

"Seriously."

"Yes. That's the day of school I must have missed."

"I'm not sure they teach it in school."

"I'm sure they have a good reason."

"School is child abuse," says Tex.

"Property is theft."

"What does that have to do with school?" asks Tex.

"I thought we were exchanging pithy sayings," I say. "But speaking of child abuse, how did you mom raise you? One emotional insight after another?"

"Something like that," says Tex. "Always urged me to pay attention to my feelings. And that being a sound member of the human community is possible: you have to work at it, but you can reach that level, and once you're there, you can stay there."

"I've never felt that," I say.

"You really don't know this stuff, do you?" asks Tex. "How our feelings come from how we perceive our situation."

"But doesn't how we perceive a situation come from our feelings?"

"Yes," says Tex.

"So it's very chicken and egg," I say.

"The point is," says Tex, "if we think we're lacking something we need to survive, we're gonna be scared. And what we think we need to survive can be almost anything, very symbolic even."

"It just sounds too much like science fiction," I say.

Three in the morning. I wake with reflux, decide to go to the campus, twelve block walk, clear my head. I imagine meeting protestors like the night Nixon went to the Lincoln Memorial. I'm about twenty yards away when the lights flicker and then it's pure abyss, darkest I've ever seen the academic world.

The blackout lasts about ten minutes, I just gaze up toward the distant heart of the universe. When the lights come on I go home and back to sleep.

Lester shows up with someone female. I get the picture: we're part of his life, bringing her is showing more of who he is, guessing he's nervous, and with reason.

Her name's Lizbeth. She's blonde, anorexic or maybe just young. I decide I'll make her a Boethius scholar.

"I've never heard of Boethius," she says.

"That's the latest in Boethius scholarship," I say, nodding approvingly.

She and Lester exchange glances. OK, he did prepare her.

Within a few minutes Tex and Lester are off to the side discussing their futures, and that leaves Lizbeth and me.

"Are you a Christer?" I ask, to break the ice.

"I don't think so," she says. "I'm Christian though."

"But not one of those fundamentalists."

"No," she says. "Why, did Lester say I was?"

"Not explicitly," I say. "Perhaps he hinted."

"Did he hint?"

"Not as such."

"Then why did you ask?"

"Because I'm having religious troubles," I say.

"Is this true, or you're just playing with me?"

OK, fully briefed.

"It's true," I say.

"What sort of troubles?"

"I've been plagued by fears of eternal damnation," I say. "Lately they're letting up a little since I started meditating. But I'm still scared. I feel like since I never created either my body or my mind, didn't launch myself so to speak, I have no idea about my future trajectory. How do you deal with such questions?"

"I'll be honest with you," she says. "I can scare myself pretty good about them, so I try to stay away."

"You and Lester happy?" I ask. Let's see what I can do.

The purest innocence comes into her eyes.

"We had this moment," she says, and she tells me about it, when it came together for them. They're attuned and I can't mess with that.

I tell Tex later.

"I knew a guy who had the same experience with a woman," he says. "They were attuned too, but he didn't have the courage a few years later and broke up with her, that's a sadness you don't want to know. Only the largeness of the universe gets him through."

Faculty party.

"Have you read Ed's latest novel?" I ask.

"No," she says, she being some professor or other, brunette. "Ed, I didn't know you were a novelist."

Ed stares at the floor.

"A vivid imagination," I say. "Emerson wrote to him welcoming him at the beginning of a great career."

"Emerson's dead," says Ed, more of a mutter, still staring at the floor.

"His dying words," I say.

"He's been dead a long time," mutters Ed. "Long before I came on the scene."

"What's the novel about?" For some reason she addresses Ed.

"It's the story," I say, "of a Robert F. Kennedy type, a politician of enormous charisma, trying to change society, except this guy isn't from a rich family. Anyway, he's running for election. Crowds flock to him, he breaks through all barriers. He's also a thinker, and he's

Alan Salant *Ablong*

given enormous thought to what he's doing."

"What happens?" she asks, turning to Ed.

"Oh, Ed's your typical writer," I say. "Does his talking in his books. But this charismatic politician understands the economic system and how his popularity's a threat to the heads of multinationals."

"What kind of threat?"

"Give us Americans something other than an immigrant past, greed, and capital-friendly religion to unite us, and there'll be no stopping us."

"There is no stopping us," she says.

"Yes, there's that," I admit. "Anyway, it turns out this politician has written a novel under a pen name, a novel that's Joyce for this new age. And he knows that if this novel gets out—"

"Yes?"

I pause for a breath, time to make up the next part.

"Well, let's just say it wouldn't play in Peoria."

"So why did he write it?"

"Ed has a long section," I say, "on the guy's powerful inner need, same reason Galileo couldn't keep his great book within the boundaries set by the Pope, had to say what was in him, the passion for truth carried him away against his conscious will. The politician's being blackmailed by a guy who knows."

"What kind of blackmail?"

"You have to read the book," I say. "But I loved his suggestion that America's current polarization is akin to the bifurcation of non-writing societies, the literarily-challenged, into factions embodying the duality underlying existence. And a great sequence about a civilization built on the sentence structure of the Nova trilogy. Oh, and the chap who finds these goggles that let him see Platonic forms within the objects they've incarnated as."

"Meaning?"

"It turns out that world peace is a small furry object currently stored, unknown to the owner, in a Houston warehouse. Let's just say the guy with the goggles is worried. And the book's a real page-turner with sex, big cocks and boobs everywhere. At one point there's even an orgy going in four rooms simultaneously, with a little leakage."

"Leakage?"

"Inter-mingling. And it isn't porn because the sex expresses each character at the deepest level, you're seeing a kind of super-organism, each dreamer's part of the dreams of everyone else, Schopenhauer in a brothel. Ed believes that as our lifespan extends we'll achieve deeper self-knowledge, Erickson's eight stages won't be enough, with time to reach new levels of consciousness we'll spill over into the ultra-human range of the spectrum. His entire orgy scene is a manifestation of this belief."

"You didn't actually write this novel," she says to Ed. He relaxes, smiles with appreciation, total gratitude. "But let me ask you something. You know how bacteria have a lending library, when one of them comes up with a gene that works, it's borrowed by the others?"

"No, actually," says Ed. Me, I'd have pretended.

"Well," she asks, "what if cells are constantly communicating in ways we don't know about—within an organism, even across organisms? And they're monitoring the planet at the cellular level—"

"And they know when something's out of balance, when something's wrong," says Ed.

"Exactly," she says. "And maybe they build structures inside us so when there are too many of us we begin to do things that doom us."

"It would explain much of modern music," I say.

"So," says Ed, "they're thinking beyond the individual being."

"Yes," she says. "Maybe for them a given organism, or even a given species, is an artificial boundary."

"Like a nation for us," says Ed.

"Yes," she says. "When will we get beyond nations?"

"I think that would be a mistake," says Ed. "Italians love being Italian, the French love being French, Americans love being American. It's family, belonging. Let the nation give us safety in childhood, but make maturity a moving beyond, to the larger world."

"I like that," she says, and I realize the conversation has left me behind, so I walk over to the salad bar, munch some broccoli.

Cardan's on my mind, did a nasty thing, stole another guy's work though there are two sides to that story, and in the process he pushed us toward truth. Artists can't be nice, truth hurts, mostly we don't want to see ourselves as we are, and when you get beyond just pretty, art is philosophy, loving truth, how we are, blemished, mortal.

Through no fault of her own, Lester's chick Lizbeth is stuck alone with me again, this time in the kitchen. She's too well-bred to leave without an excuse, and evidently so far nothing's come to mind.

"But what if the worst is true?"

"The worst of what?"

"It doesn't matter."

"Well, then, all I can do is hope it isn't," she says. "Just like I hope

I won't get pancreatic cancer."

"The other side is that I've had some new religious thoughts," I say. "Want to hear them?"

She looks nervously toward the room where Tex and Lester are still discussing their futures.

"I'm a little tired," she says. "Late night. Maybe another time."

I take that as a green light.

"Imagining that the world's run by a mind that's not perhaps perfect opens a whole new range of thoughts," I say. "And I'm hoping that if it's run by the traditional God he won't hold it against me that I imagine such a possibility. I tell myself he wouldn't be so petty, but I don't know if at that level it isn't pettiness."

"Let's all hope," says Lizbeth, looking away.

"Now suppose fissures open in the consciousness of that mind and that's why nature's red in tooth and claw and why Hitler gets rejected by painting school."

"There are many births that, at least to outward appearance, are to be regretted," she says.

"Or maybe," I say, "in the land of multiple universes, all born and reared under a Darwinian sun, so to speak, with black holes as the wombs, God the Creator is training apprentices, or subcontracts out certain universes, ours being one."

"There are days it feels like that," she says.

"I imagine," he says, "a new civilization rising in the shadow of a belief in this different God."

Now she's actually looking at me.

"Of a God that means well," she says, "always does mean well, but maybe makes mistakes."

"And regrets them. Prayer services include moments of compassion, feeling for the guy. He's like one's parents viewed from the perspective of adulthood, instead of a six-month-old's vision."

"I know what you mean," she says.

Actually I'm not sure I do, at least about the parents.

"All I'm saying," I continue, "is that there's a middle position between belief and atheism."

"You mean agnosticism."

"No. Suppose that God is the best of humanity, but flawed. And we're his children."

"The best in what way?"

"The smartest, funniest, most creative, a hyper-Shakespeare, ten million gazillion times Shakespeare. And God in shaping our universe has the pure joy of creation, he revels in the incredible beauty and interest and intricacy, including these self-aware beings."

"What about the bad stuff?"

"See, that's the point," I say. "God has a conscience and he feels really terrible about evil. And he's not quite smart enough to figure out a universe where there isn't suffering. So he goes around in disguise, asks his creatures whether they're glad they exist, or does the bad stuff make them wish they'd never been born, hatched, etc."

"How does he speak to them?"

"In dream," I say, "or deeper levels of unconsciousness, places that know no lying, a universal language he implanted within us all. And he gets his answer, and I'm guessing it's a resounding Yes, glad to be here, though maybe if he interviews a deer being dismembered by a lion, there's hesitation."

Seems everybody knows me, so when someone shows up who doesn't, it's exciting. At the University Store a young guy comes up to me.

"Do you work here?" he asks.

"As little as possible," I say.

"I mean, do you work at the store?"

I'm tempted, but that identity doesn't appeal to me.

"No," I say. "I'm actually a self-help guru. I've written a book that's on its way to best-sellerdom, it's gonna help a lot of people."

"What's your secret?"

"You have to buy the book," I say.

"Where can I find it?"

"Oh, it isn't out yet," I say. "Next month."

"What's it called?"

"It's called Finding Your Inner Asshole."

"Unusual title."

"It's an unusual book," I say.

"Can you give me a clue?"

"I recommend that you open a store that sells Certainty," I say. "Call it the Certainty Store."

"People do like certainty," he says.

I'm ready to stop but something keeps me talking to him.

"I can tell you one thing," I say. "At any moment of your life, visualize the best of yourself. Think of the moments when you've been most alive, when you've been firing on all cylinders."

"Thanks," he says. "Can you give me one more?"

I like the guy. Young innocence, eagerness. The whole male thing confuses me, there's a bunch of these lanky healthy good-self-esteem

Alan Salant *Ablong*

eager young guys out there, they attract women not by macho, not by posing, not even by sensitivity, but by eagerness and good intentions. One look and you know they want to make a good world, and they think they can do it, but not from vanity, because they're not vain. I know this guy without having met him. He sees the good in people, and somehow I don't want to mess him up.

"Ever read James Clerk Maxwell?"

"The scientist?"

"Yeah."

"No. He wrote, well, science, didn't he? Equations and stuff? Not easy."

"Read about him," I say. "He had a beautiful philosophy of life. He viewed each day in the context of his entire life, sought its meaning in that perspective."

"You're not the typical self-help guru," the kid says.

No, I think, I'm not. We stand there in awkward silence for a moment.

"I think you've chosen the wrong title," he says.

Tex is in a bad mood when I get home.

"What's eating you?" I ask.

"You really let me down as a father," he says.

"You're just realizing that?"

"In a way, yes," he says.

"And what do you expect me to do about it?"

"Take it like a man," he says.

"Take what like a man?"

We're standing, facing each other, and then he throws a punch to my jaw, and I'm on the ground.

"Get up," he says.

"I'm actually more comfortable down here," I say.

"Up."

I stand up and he decks me again, another part of jaw. Kid's got a good punch.

"You've made your point," I say.

"Up."

I stand up again and he hits my jaw for the third time and down I go.

"You may not realize it," I say, "but this actually hurts. How many more times are you planning to do this?"

"I think I'm done," he says. "I think that's what I needed."

"I'm glad," I say, standing up, and now I punch his jaw, a really good punch, learned it in the unpopularity and aloneness of childhood, and he's down.

"What was that for?" he asks.

"I dislike being punched," I say.

The next morning we don't look so good, head to the infirmary, explain we fought off an attack by a bunch of positivists.

"It was eight of them," I say. "You should see what those guys look like."

"Are you ready to tell me what really caused your scar?" Jume asks.

"Not particularly," I say.

"Give it a try anyway."

"I should have gone to a non-directive therapist," I say.

"Bad luck," she says.

"All right," I say. I feel sudden dread as searing pain along my neck, eyes, and forehead, and fear riding the monorail of my spine. "It was when I was almost eight. I had a brain operation."

"Broccoli truth?"

"Yes," I say. That's our measure now. If she asks if it's broccoli level of truth, I can refuse to answer, but if I say yes, it means yes, it's true.

"Just before your eighth birthday," she says.

All academics is abuzz, huge discovery in Baghdad just a few miles from where Saddam was born and brutalized into a brutalizer.

It started with a suicide bombing, explosion exposed a ridge no one had noticed, an archaeologist descends and finds Babylonian writings different from what anyone expected, turns out they beat the Greeks to a lot of stuff, a previously unknown philosophical tradition, the whole history of civilization's gonna have to be rewritten.

"I knew it never sounded right," I tell Ed.

"You never mentioned it," he says.

"I didn't want to keep you up nights," I say.

Therapy: all that just talking's a waste, as if words matter. The world doesn't stop while you realize something about yourself, who has the time? You fall behind.

"I find it interesting," says Jume, "that your broccoli visions began so soon after your operation."

"I suppose."

"That's all?" she asks.

"What else do you want?"

"You have no feelings about it?"

"My life isn't that important," I say, and that feels true, and painful beyond the pain I'm used to, as I say it. "It happened, why dwell on it?"

"Some therapists might call that resistance," says Jume.

"Luckily you're not one of them, right?"

"You had a brain operation and soon after you began seeing beings who occupy the central places of the universe."

"I don't know what you want of me," I say.

"Since when do you care what I want of you?"

"It's just an expression."

"You have no thoughts on the subject?"

"Do you want me to say that maybe something went really wrong in that operation, and that I've been crazy ever since? That my brain is making up a story that only tells the nature of its disease?"

"Something like that. And also, I'm wondering if—" And she says something that pushes me over the edge.

I rise from my chair and lunge at her, hands around her neck, her eyes are bugging out of her head.

"This isn't therapeutic," she whispers in a strangled voice. "This isn't therapeutic. This isn't therapeutic."

I let go because it suddenly seems funny to me, the way she's saying it. I get up and go back to my seat.

She's stunned and then furious. She goes through a bunch of motions, rearranges her hair, like she's trying to put herself back together again.

"I really am so sorry," I say, drawing out the 'so' along a full exhalation that involves a lot of my body. "Are you OK?"

"I don't know yet," she says. "That was assault. I want you to leave. I'll call you if I think I can ever work with you again."

That night in bed my head's disintegrating, more thoughts in an hour than I've had in entire years, unsuspected connections among the many parts of my life. Categories that never fit are interlocking, finding their place, like when that guy studied a map and realized Africa and South America looked like former lovers.

The next day I'm lecturing on Quantum Aerobics as it relates to the German philosophers, and five minutes in I just start talking about myself. You could hear a pin drop, and I don't mean it as a metaphor. Someone dropped a bobby pin and everybody heard the sound and turned.

When I get home I leave Jume a message with my apology, ask if we can do sessions on the phone, laptop, webcam. She calls back and

says that's fine, she just needs a few weeks so her desire to drop a gre-
nade on my head can subside.

I'm sitting with Rhyth at the kitchen table. He jumps up.

"What?" I ask.

"Wrong room," he says. "We need to talk in the living-room."

"Need to," I say. "In what sense? Can you locate it in Maslow's
hierarchy of needs?"

"I'm not kidding," he says. "There's something I have to tell you,
and I can't tell you in here."

"Why not?"

"Because I don't know it in here."

I grab some broccoli from the refrigerator just in case, while Rhyth
hurls himself at the living-room floor and sprawls.

"Is that Pilates?" I ask.

"I just feel comfortable this way."

"OK," I say. "What's the big secret? Are you an illegal immigrant?"

"I don't know yet," says Rhyth.

"You don't know if you're an illegal immigrant?"

"No," says Rhyth, "I don't know what I have to tell you."

"Do we need another room?" I ask, fingering the broccoli.

"It's a feeling, it'll come," he says, gets thoughtful. "Tell me something—"

"Sure," I say. "There's a theory that the body carries on an ongoing
inner conversation, bone talking to bone, nerve to nerve. Most of us
don't hear it, but in autistic people the brain converts it into words so
it's like they're always at a crowded cocktail party—"

"Where is this coming from?"

"I don't have the reference at hand," I say.

"No, I mean, why are you telling me this?"

"You asked me to tell you something."

"When I said 'tell me something,'" says Rhyth, "that was actually
intended as the opening, the preamble, to a question I wanted to ask you."

"Intention's so pre-911," I say, "so pre-Freudian. Some say
thought is blocked action: each time an action's interrupted you have
a thought. In sleep our muscles are paralyzed and that's when our
minds flood with dreams—"

I watch Rhyth debate whether to accept his loss of control of the
conversation.

"So that in a fully free society there'd be less thinking?" he asks.

"I don't know," I say, "but the French psychotherapist Lacan would

Alan Salant *Ablong*

end sessions abruptly because truncated thought brings break-throughs. And Freud spoke of negative hallucinations—"

"What?"

"You hypnotize a guy, tell him there's no furniture in the room, then snap him out and ask him to get something from the far end. Know what happens?"

"No."

"He'll take a path that avoids the furniture, though if you ask him he'll insist there isn't any furniture, he'll invent excuses for his indirect route—"

"That's it, that's exactly it," says Rhyth. "Imagine that Levi-Strauss is right and there's wild thought underlying society, a bedrock non-rational syntax. And imagine a person who suddenly experiences the world through that syntax, and in an instant all social structures make sense—"

"I think the experiment's failed," I say.

"You mean Western civilization's effort to build knowledge by reason?"

"No," I say, "I mean going into the living room. I'm hungry, and that's a conversation best held in the kitchen."

"Wait," says Rhyth. "This is what I wanted to tell you."

"Go ahead."

"No, I just said it."

"What you wanted to tell me is 'no, wait, this is what I wanted to tell you'?"

Rhyth's too agitated to be deterred.

"Don't you get it?" he asks. "Speaking that syntax, the person knows why we have religion, why we have lotteries, bars, all of it. In an extraordinary series of intuitions he sees the otherwise invisible lines connecting each aspect of society. Like seeing a worldwide river system and suddenly understanding why cities are where they are. This syntax makes it immediately clear why some things exist and others don't, why we follow certain practices and not others—"

"It reminds me," I say, and I see him flinch, "of the metaphor for curved space, watching people with lanterns at night moving in strange paths, by day you see the hill they've been climbing and it all makes sense—"

"The puzzlement of a child," says Rhyth, "is the result of not seeing the central river system, and thus coming up with explanations far from actuality, ideas that guide his actions and his whole life but don't work. And why they don't work is only understandable in terms of their distance from the actual workings of the river system."

"And if someone sees the system," I say, "or intuits it—"

"He'll do well in life, a mystery to those who don't perceive the system. And all kinds of irrelevant associations may be made—to a particular philosophy, for instance—leaving us puzzled why some people who are living that philosophy succeed and others fail. But a person who could produce a vision in others of the river system—"

"Would be a great teacher."

"Yes."

"Suppose," I say, "there's a language that makes this vision natural, explains what perhaps exists below or at an angle to the level of words. And if this language became known and genuinely accessible—a musical language perhaps, or painting, or math, or the equivalent for the Unconscious of math—"

"Then," says Rhyth, "we'd lead lives filled with purpose, clear pursuit of what we most deeply need—"

"And the straight lines, the shortest paths, the geodesics of this life would be the actions that bring direct fulfillment, corresponding to the underlying river systems."

"Yes. And a society which evolved to be visible, in which for example institutions of power and control no longer mystified, would produce people who—"

"One thing's unclear to me," I say.

"What?

"Why couldn't you say this in the kitchen?"

"So you're not pressing charges?" I ask.

"No," says Jume, safe on the other end of the screen.

"What do I do now?"

"As before," she says. "Except if you lunge this time, it just means you've got a broken computer. What got you so angry?"

"I think it was something you said," I say.

"I mean specifically."

"I've always been horrified by the thought that I'm just crazy. My brain's just diseased, maybe even Quantum Aerobics is merely a symptom."

"And how do you feel saying that?"

Stunned, actually. Like the thread holding the sword of Damocles just turned into a lo mein noodle. My brain's what it is, and QA does what it does, and I feel muscles relaxing all over my body.

I'm now going freeform from the lectern. I scrap my talk on QA and the roots of mathematics. Rules are dropping, students shouting

Alan Salant *Ablong*

out questions, coming up to the microphone, it's a free-for-all.

"Can QA be applied to compute what globalization is, whether it's helping or not, who it's helping?" asks one.

"I don't know," I say. "It never occurred to me."

Lectures run over, students suggesting ideas, professors come from everywhere like when Weierstrass began teaching mathematical analysis and the future of the field unfolded in his classroom, all magic, I didn't know it could be like this.

Lester grabs me after class.

"I didn't know you had this in you, man," he says. "I always wondered why you taught when you don't have to."

Me too: what pleasure kept me showing up? Hope of an experience like this?

I extend the course into summer, root of a new kind of social science.

"It could be your second great breakthrough," says Bud from literature, in a good mood, his Kesey lectures are a hit.

"It wouldn't be mine," I say. "The ideas are coming from, well, everyone."

Very nervously I go back on broccoli.

"Any thoughts about why you?" asks Jume.

"Well," I say, "we've mentioned the brain operation. And there's this daydream I had. An odd discovery's made about a remote fish, it has a receptor that receives along an ignored and overgrown byway of the electromagnetic spectrum. This receptor appears from time to time along the tree of life, and it's in me. It was developed for other purposes."

"What did it do for the fish?"

"How would I know?" I ask.

"I thought maybe in your daydream—"

"The daydream wasn't under my conscious control," I say. "It followed its own logic. Perhaps the fish lacked the intellectual equipment to convert the received information into knowable form. Or maybe it experienced it as an urge to modify its evolutionary path."

"Meaning?"

"When I was working out the math for Quantum Aerobics, I noticed that the good old Fibonacci sequence kept peeking out from within the genetic forms. What seem like random mutations are actually governed by mathematical patterns, almost an iron law—"

"So life is following a path laid down before its existence."

"Maybe," I say.

"We were talking recently about your operation," she says. "How did you feel back then?"

"I notice you changed the subject."

"I want to complete our work while we're alive," she says. "How did you feel?"

"Like a freak," I say. "Something wrong with my brain, they had to fix it." Feelings rise, OK, I'll honor them. "Or like a homely girl who perks up as those secondary sex characteristics kick in, now all the guys want her, but inside it's still all ugly feeling."

"I don't understand," she says.

"I thought something was wrong with my brain," I say. "That I was a moron. And then suddenly I found out I was pretty smart. But the stupid feeling stays."

"So you're ashamed."

The answer is yes, but I don't really want to say it. I imagine a new kind of therapy where you make progress by denying everything.

"What's going on in you?" she asks.

"I feel like if I admit the shame, then all the rest comes with it."

"The rest of what?"

"I don't know where to start."

"Anywhere," she says.

So I tell her, and it shocks the hell out of me—that I put all this distance between myself and other people because of shame, that I like to make people feel stupid because I feel stupid, that dammit, my son's right, I could really enjoy this life I've been given. That one really gets me. Just by living it?

"And?"

I can walk into any room and people are ready to thank me for saving someone they know, and all I do is just try to make them feel stupid. And I never put it together, never realized that the feeling just before wanting to make them feel stupid is my shame. Like having erections around sexy women and not realizing the erection comes from seeing sexy women.

I look out at what had been a cloudy day and it's all sun, world in tune with me, I love that pathetic fallacy. And behind the clouds the sun was always there.

She's smiling inside the computer beside an ad for condoms that somehow just popped up on my screen.

"Am I cured?"

"I doubt it," she says. "But you've just learned something important, I think. How does that feel?"

How does it feel? Like a revolution inside my head, the new government's already in place and they're good guys. And a soft warmth

Alan Salant *Ablong*

toward Jume that's a new feeling for me, and I know why so many people said she's just the best there is.

I tell Tex the whole session, almost word for word what I said to her. And it takes longer than the session itself because I stumble, repeat myself, add commentary.

Tex listens patiently.

"What do you think?" I ask.

"Sounds about right," he says, gets up, goes outside.

My first time back on broccoli I can see all the way around the guy's head and I'm seeing his thoughts—like it's extra-dimensional and everything's visible inside him—and a different kind of inside, which is mind. Thinking's simply an extra dimension, a different way I couldn't imagine.

I'm seeing through his eyes to the center of the universe, why me? And as I stare at the center of the universe there's something very familiar there.

He turns toward me, the guy whose eyes I saw through, and he asks: satisfied?

I want more, sure, but yes, I'm satisfied too, I've never been satisfied before. The idea that it might be a benign universe, that it might be good enough, is new to me. But it soon fades, except for the thought that maybe these galaxies are the structure of my thought.

I feel the need to talk to someone but Tex isn't here and Lester's been around less lately, empty cot, did he move out?

Ed, bless his soul, stops by again.

"We were just talking about you," I say.

"Oh?" His eyes light up.

"I was telling Tex about your new four-dimensional GPS, zip codes including time so you can set the device for past or future. Drawbacks, sure, sometimes it drops you in a space-time desert, real wasteland—gotta be specific, the BJs in Tenafly 3 PM June 4, 2015. Unfortunately it won't come standard—standard GPS will handle only space—but for a little extra you get full 4D functionality."

"I never had such an idea," says Ed.

"Are you sure?"

My house phone rings, an actual call, answer to an ad I placed in the campus newspaper. 'Assistance with plots at low cost. Will help any writer get any character from point A to point B. Also available to governments and corporations for real-world plotting.'

"Just a joke," I say.

"Oh," says the guy, and something on the other end makes me very nervous.

Tex holds up my copy of Kierkegaard's *Philosophical Fragments*.

"Reading this?" he asks.

"Yes," I say.

"Anything in particular that strikes you?"

"Yes," I say, surprised, the offspring still wants to know me. "You'll find a post-it marking the paragraph."

He finds it, reads aloud. "'*But what is this unknown something with which the Reason collides when inspired by its paradoxical passion, with the result of unsettling even man's knowledge of himself?*'"

"Why that passage?" he asks.

"I'm not sure," I say, and his question initiates in me a new train of thought. "But I have this idea I wanted to talk about."

"Test it out," he says, when I've told him. "Tell people. Scientific method and all that."

"Tell which people?"

"Tell your class."

So I go up extempore, just start spouting. Lately class has been packed, we've moved to the biggest hall on campus where they usually hold the freshman survey classes that nobody can get out of.

"For instance," I'm saying, "you have periods where a whole process is summarized quickly. Algebra takes centuries to go from verbal to symbolic, one halting step after another. But Boole takes logic from words to symbols in a decade, telescopes the history of math in one short career. Can we do the same for emotions?"

"Impossible," shouts some turd of a kid.

"Shut up," says a very pretty girl in the front, patron of the arts, appreciates genius. "Let the professor speak. He's a lot smarter than you are."

"I think we can," I say, "and here's how. Suppose Erickson's right about his eight stages. I believe he says at each stage half the people make it through, the other half don't. Suppose you can skip stages, do stage 3 and 7 but not the rest."

"That's impossible," shouts another bed-wetter. "If you can't deal with separation from mom, you can't do anything else."

"Why not?"

"If you can't feel safe with her, you've got nothing safe to compare the rest of the world to, so you can't get safe with the world. And then the other stages are unreachable."

"But let's posit that you can," I say. "And you get a one for each

Alan Salant *Ablong*

stage you pass, a zero otherwise. So a guy who's mastered stages three, five, and seven is 00101010. And there's an algebra for when two people get together, how their numbers combine, that's the two-person problem, like Newton's two-body problem. The n-person problem's more complex."

"So what?"

"Remember," I say, "how folks learned about individual elements, but then Mendeleev drew it all together with his periodic table? We await our Mendeleev. With this binary scheme you can take the DSM-V or whatever number they're at now and begin classifying in real groupings. And maybe there's a proper drug or psychotherapy or religion for each group, read a person's psych number and you know what he needs. Make it a science."

The next day I get a note from the psych department.

Dear Professor Ablong,

You're ignorant about psychology. Please stop misleading students about our field.

Sincerely,

The Entire Psychology Department

"Remove the broccoli from your life," says Jume, "and what do you have left? You OK so far?"

"Yep."

"Perhaps it's like removing God, a radical procedure," she says.

"How are they similar?"

"Because for many people God is the entryway to the benevolence of the human heart, the love within the human race. And that's what broccoli does for you. Take them away—you OK?"

"Yep."

"Take them away—"

"Face the benevolence alone."

"Exactly," she says. "And just as in your famous theorem, what you've taken away you can then put back in."

"You know about my theorem?"

"I saw an episode of *Nova*," she says.

"I sued them over that episode," I say.

"Why?"

"They quoted me out of context."

"About what?"

"The third law of Quantum Aerobics."

"How did they misquote you?"

"They said nothing about the crapper," I say.

"And you sued them."

"Yes."

"For money?"

"Interesting," I say. "What other possibilities are there?"

"I think we're getting far afield here," she says. "What frightens you about seeing the love in your own heart?"

"That's what you say is going on."

"If some aspect of us is associated with searing pain, welcoming it home happens in stages. And one stage is inventing an entity to hold feelings we can't yet feel because of that pain. Entire institutions exist to do that in societies that reject key parts of being human due to historical trauma."

"That's how I see the Department of Motor Vehicles," I say.

"Stay with this," she says. "Maybe all humanity is part of a process where one day we can really let go. Did you really have your breakthrough on the crapper?"

"Why do you ask that?"

"Just a hunch."

She's good with her hunches.

"I'm not sure I want to talk about it," I say

"I think you'll feel better if you do. Give it a try."

"It happened," I say, and it isn't easy, "my first time."

"First time?"

"I was a virgin 'til I was twenty-one," I say.

"And?"

"Just as I was coming I had this feeling, and as I lay beside her after, that feeling enveloped me and with it ideas in a kaleidoscopic flash, and suddenly I knew." That disappointment with women after: waiting for another breakthrough every single time, what I hoped for.

"Right then and there."

"It took five months to get it right," I say. "Sleeping two hours a night, eating just to keep my body going, chewing felt like a waste of time. Just read, think, work out the math. And that feeling, that moment, was my steady light, I never lost sight of where I was or what I was heading toward."

"This is a side of you that you don't talk about very often," she says.

I'm crying, and that night I dream a wind-stirred lake, currents and flows so complex that the entire history of life's within it, forms on the ancient banks pressing their imprint on the water, and we have to live with all of it, and it isn't fair. And then the sheer beauty of the lake hits me, o my God.

Alan Salant *Ablong*

The Chaotics arrive on campus. They started as a rock band, made it big, tired of music, became a cult, tired of being a cult, became nomads visiting the places young folks gather, now they've poured music back into the mix, just went platinum. I'm stuck on the dais next to the band leader who's modestly taken the stage name Song. We're raising money for something, and Tex promised it would be good for my soul.

"Everything has to be expressed," Song answers, though I hadn't asked anything. "If this guy doesn't do it, then someone else has to."

"What are we talking about here?" I ask.

"Murder, genius, every perversity. The human community must be whole, the entire psyche must breathe."

"So it's not just Jesus dying for our sins."

"No," says Song. "If nobody's playing the rogue, the whole inner pulse is wrong and we feel it, and finally someone will step up."

"So Hitler's taking one for the team," I say.

"Yes."

"All interconnected, everything participates in everything else, we're all one."

"Exactly," says Song, nudges his drummer. "Got an idea for a ditty."

"What were you doing just before you had your big idea?" asks Jume.

"I already told you about the sex," I say. "Want more details? A bit of the voyeur, I see."

"I mean more generally," she says, rolls her eyes. "The day before, the week before."

"Sexually?"

"Not just sex," she says. "Your life as a whole."

"Oh," I say. "Oh."

"What?"

"I never focused like I did in that period. Reading and writing and thinking fourteen, fifteen hours a day. When I concentrate I can pour in a lot of information quickly, at least I could back then. For a few years I'd been absorbing every idea I could find."

"What sorts of ideas?"

"Math first: analysis, algebra, topology, and chaos theory which was pretty new then, anything on morphology. Of course physics. And depth psychology, mythology, literature."

"What kinds of literature?"

"All the experimental writers I could find, anybody who was wide open. And the sort of criticism that shows literature as our lives. Art history, genetics, structuralism."

"All of that."

"And in that first, well, sexual experience, that first love experience—I never quite thought of it this way—"

"It all seemed to come together."

She understands me, that moment.

"What did you mean last time," I ask, "when you said it's a side of me I seldom show?"

"How desperately you seek truth, you, how hard you've worked."

I didn't think truth existed or that I had a right to it or that it extended to my life, pursued it incognito, snuck up on it without letting myself know, hid my hunger.

Tex is sprawled in the living room, filling the couch.

"All of life is questions," I say.

"How so?" asks Tex.

"See what I mean?"

"No, just give it to me straight."

"Girl I knew," I say, "daughter of a Holocaust survivor, goes to an art museum, sees *The Scream*, starts crying, wailing, lets out everything in her."

"What's that got to do with questions?"

"The painting was the answer to a question she hadn't asked, hadn't known to ask. Watch a committee at work, your average jerks in a room. They set out to solve a problem, wouldn't know the answer if it grabbed their cocks."

"So?"

"What's their problem?"

"How should I know? You didn't tell me."

"I mean in general."

"The human condition."

"Less general than that."

"I give up."

"It's that they're not all trying to answer the same question."

"How so?"

"One guy's seeking mother-love, another's after father-love, another's enacting a sibling rivalry, the guy running the meeting's still researching whether the world's safe."

"OK."

"Therapy's job is to find the questions you're asking, and the first step's realizing that you're asking questions and the world's sending answers. And the questions take the form of how we live, situations we enter. And the answers are how people respond to us. But because we don't know the question we're asking, we don't recognize that what happens to us is the answer."

"An example?"

"I wondered once how long I'd known Ed, how long he'd suffered. And the next day I recalled our first conversation, it was about the 2005 London subway bombings. But I didn't remember wondering how long I'd known Ed."

"So you didn't realize why the memory came."

"Right."

"When these answers come to us—"

"See, that's the thing," I say. It's dawning on me that feeling connected to humanity means I want to make things better, this is kind of cool. "The answer comes in a snatch of a song, how light hits a garbage can, what someone says to us. But we misinterpret."

"We react to it on its own terms instead of seeing that it's an answer."

"And maybe at some level we know, and our reaction is stronger because of that."

"And if whenever you react surprisingly strongly you write it down, look at the list periodically for patterns—"

"Yes," I say.

"*What Color is Your Parachute.*"

"I don't currently own a parachute," I say.

"No," he says. "The book. Finding your calling by reviewing your whole life."

"Oh."

"So let's sum up," says Tex. "You didn't care about anyone, then you had a crisis of faith, you got scared about what God was going to do to you when you were dead and couldn't fight back with your body because you didn't have one, and now you're starting to care. Have I got it?"

"Pretty much," I say.

"I'll be right back," he says, goes into the other room, I think he calls someone.

The broccolite who's befriended me sends smoke rings my way, and they turn into words.

"What kind of life form are you?" I ask.

"Life?" he asks.

"Aren't you life?"

86

"No, we're not." I see them conversing, they look like a benzene ring right now, snake swallowing its tail, I see a page of a book of symbols listing all the mythic meanings of that shape.

"Have you…encountered life?"

"I think so," I say. "I mean, I'm alive."

"You? You're alive?"

Another benzene ring. I become frightened they'll squeeze the universe out of existence.

"We've heard of life," he says, returning. "There are old rumors. But we never knew if they were true."

"What else is there? Are you death?"

"No, not death."

We get into a long discussion. The smoke rings make me cough so it's a little time between words.

"We want to learn from you," he says.

"Learn what?"

Images beyond my control, dreamy but other, burst from a place so deep that intellect and emotions merge, root linking the awareness of all life, how thought began. Exhausting: I tell him I need to sleep.

"Sleep? What's that?"

I try explaining the difference between sleep and waking and he just can't seem to get it. Doesn't help that we're now communicating in a series of strobe flashes that are somehow also words, is that what disco was about? And moments like being underwater after you've used your final stored breath.

Afterwards I stay away for a month. I don't know if they live in time.

She's tall, ill from cancer, very thin. Tex's mom, her name's Doreen, he drove me to a beach to meet her. My ten-day affair.

"Mom, meet Dad."

"I do remember you," I say.

"Well, that's something, I guess." A hollowness of disease surrounds her eyes.

"I liked you," I say.

Doreen turns her full eye-attention to me, and I can sense that something important, rehearsed many times, is happening. She has to explain to herself how so crucial a part of her life involved me.

"Did you really?"

"I don't say something like that if I don't mean it," I say. "I've never allowed myself to be forced into emotional dishonesty. Even my lies are truth."

Alan Salant *Ablong*

"In some ways you haven't changed," says Doreen.

"He's changed," says Tex, a little too eagerly, jumping in. Not his usual mellow: he's got something at stake here, a lot. "He's changed in the short time I've known him."

A breeze from the south brings chatter of birds. The sun's edged by cloud fronds that make it a blazing flower. In the ocean kids squeal with delight, back to the water, let's all go back to the water, declare the last few hundred million years of evolution a mistake, back on more liquid biological ground.

I think the ocean's suited for Communism, check what economic system the dolphins use. Who knows what else is going on in the water?

"Look, let's get it over with," I say. "You hate me, blah blah blah, I left you with this kid, blah blah blah. You realize I didn't know, and you never bothered to tell me?"

Doreen bends her body slowly and sits on the large red blanket that we've spread across ridges of sand.

"He was way better off without you," she says.

"I have no doubt," I say. "And we've made up for lost time. Tex is quite a nudge, you know."

"Who's Tex?"

"I told you," says Tex. "Remember the thing about the names?"

"Right, right, I forgot."

"Thanks for loving our son," I say.

It's a paradoxical intervention and it throws her off guard, buys me a moment or two.

"Do you really mean that?"

"I do," I say, getting in as much sympathy per syllable as I can. I can't insult as well when I'm dealing with cancer so I have to adjust my tactics, it's Sun Tzu.

"I just want us, for a few minutes, to be a family," says Tex.

"Shall we show you how we made you?" I ask.

We go to a restaurant by the ocean. I'm reading the soups and imagine ordering a bowl of ocean, heck, the whole ocean with all the sea-creatures inside, almost forget I'm vegetarian.

"You must be really hungry," says Tex.

"Are you reading my mind now?" I ask.

"No," he says. "Your eyes get really big when you're hungry."

I gaze at the water as it washes the lights that fall on it from the shore. Ignoring all the murders underneath that crystal surface I feel peaceful. And the sky's a beautiful bass blue deepening to the black ink with which Night will write Tomorrow.

"Who are you actually?" Doreen asks me.

"Although I'm the father of your child," I say, "I can see he's really a good kid. Whatever you did, it worked."

Doreen smiles from her hollowed eyes, the fatigue in them, trying to complete the puzzle of her life. I do feel sad.

"There must be something in you too," she says, "for you to find such depth of meaning inside a simple vegetable."

I turn betrayed to Tex.

"You told her about the broccoli?"

"It's what made up her mind to come," he says.

"We'll be talking about this," I say to Tex, and fear flashes in his eyes, a rarity.

"Why did you come?" I ask Doreen.

"Completion," she says.

"I know that," I say. "I mean, the real reason."

"Completion is the real reason."

"You're better than that," I say. "The real real reason."

She sighs. "I miss you."

That calls for a response.

"Did you really try to abort Tex?"

"Ah," she says. "Why do you ask?"

"Because he really doesn't seem to be angry at you."

"I told him to tell you a fib," she says.

"Why?"

"So all this would happen."

I've never been so scared of a human being before.

She comes home with us. She sleeps on my bed, long sleep, so tired. I open a cot for myself in the living room, Tex snores in the guest room.

The next morning I ask Doreen. "The mentoring thing was your idea too?"

"Yep," she says. Looks a little better, sleep helped her.

"Are you really able to produce human outcomes?" I ask.

"With certain kinds of people," she says.

"Well," I ask, "if you know that much, can't you defeat death?"

I know it's a stupid comment, but at that moment it made sense to me.

"It doesn't work that way," she says. "Even if we get this whole thing figured out, emotions and all, we'll still be mortals."

"I'm not so sure," I say. "There's been some good research lately."

Alan Salant *Ablong*

"It won't come in time for me, anyway."

All right, enough about her.

"What do I need?" I ask.

"You need to look at yourself from outside yourself," she says.

"And what about you?" I ask, surprising myself. "What do you need?"

"Wow," she says. "Tex was right. You have changed."

"What do you mean?"

That sadness is in her eyes again, and I got it now. Something could have worked between us if I'd been a few decades, maybe a few centuries, more mature.

She can see that I know exactly what she meant, we're communicating wordlessly the way I communicate with the broccolites.

"What did you feel toward me?" she asks.

I tell her. I tell about the two hundred eighty women I've actually slept with, every single one was a one-night stand except her. A vast magnetic repelling force, a terror of intimacy, always pulling me away, and yet the something we had together was powerful enough to keep me coming back for, well, ten days.

"This is truth?" she asks.

I nod.

"Wow," she says.

"Why?"

"Because I thought so. I thought something was there. I dreamt you were a baby crying out to me."

"There's no need to get insulting."

"I was so sad when you left."

She leaves, returns a few weeks later, Tex picks her up, she can barely move. We get her into bed.

She dies the next morning.

"What the fuck?" I ask.

It turns out Tex hadn't told me the full story.

"She kind of, well, stopped the treatments," he says.

"Stopped the treatments? What, because of cost? I could have paid—"

"Not the cost," he says.

"Of course I could've paid the cost."

"I mean, it's not because of the cost that she—"

"A kind of suicide, then."

"They weren't worth it any more," says Tex. "Too much pain."

And so she died in my bed.

That night I can't sleep, in a real dark place. Death, the unknown, what do we do? I imagine word gets out that bad things are on the other side, now everybody freaks, we're heading for the gears of a malicious machine and we know it, smart cows in a slaughterhouse but worse, how do we help each other, anything we can do? Group cohesion worked with big frightening animals, but this? All you have to do to stop a soccer match, theatrical production, day at school, is say: 'guys, we know what's coming.'

The next day Tex talks about her a lot, hours. At the very end she read a book of the surviving fragments of the pre-Socratic philosophers, and that's what decided her on dying.

"The book was that bad?" I ask.

A few weeks in which, to my surprise, I mourn, sadness I didn't know was inside me, was it her departing soul that put it there? Tex wants to take care of the funeral process—scattering ashes—but I find myself saying I'll do it; something in me died with her.

What, exactly? Try my therapist, she'll have ideas.

"What did she mean to you?" she asks.

"I don't see where that'll lead," I say.

"Just talk about it," she says. "Talking will tell us what she means to you, and then we'll understand."

"I still don't see why talking should work," I say.

"Our psyches are largely constructed with our thoughts and ideas. We're built of what things mean to us."

"Prove it," I say.

"I can't," she says. "So what did she mean to you?"

Maybe I did love her, maybe there's a reason she had my kid.

The talk of the campus is how a stray elk has arrived. Everybody comes out to see it.

"How did it get here?" asks Lester, stopping by one evening.

"You know the circus that visited just down the road?"

"No."

"That's where the elk came from."

"They don't have elks in circuses," says Lester.

"It is surprising on many levels," I admit.

The elk tours the campus, people figure out what to feed it, and it seems happy. One day it makes its way into calculus class. The professor tries to keep going, but calculus can't compete with a live elk.

Alan Salant *Ablong*

The professor proves the mean-value theorem to no one. I tell Tex.

"You have bigger fish to fry," says Tex.

"What?"

"You have amends to make, 12-step stuff, *My Name is Earl*, all of it."

"What do you mean?"

"Fix what you've broken."

"Why?"

"Don't you want to?"

"I'm an angry orphan," I say. "I never got what I needed. I want the right to break anything I want to, because the world broke me."

"For real?"

"Maybe," I say. Maybe.

At this simple place in me it really is that, I want to break things, and it's so naïve, childish, reduces the world.

So I make my list, step one is telling the dean to go on his walkabout.

"Thanks," he says. "I'm going tomorrow."

"You don't have to be swayed by me quite that dramatically," I say.

"I booked the trip two months ago, you idiot," he says.

Are they allowed to call a Nobel Prize winner an idiot these days? Who's to know what is and isn't OK? Is it written somewhere?

"Why are you looking at me like that?" asks Tex.

"I didn't realize I was."

"Well, you are."

"Am I still?"

"Sort of, yeah."

"OK," I say. "I want you to explain yourself. Tell me who you are. I don't know how a person like you is made, and since Doreen's dead she's not going to be telling me, I think. So explain."

"What sort of person am I?"

"That's what I'm asking."

"No, I mean, what sort of person do you believe me to be?"

"You're light-years beyond me in consciousness. You're playing the game at a different level, you're just so many steps ahead of me. Why did you come here?"

"You know."

"There should be a class," I say. "Early in school, maybe third grade. You can go up to anybody that you can see has answers you don't, and just ask: how did you get to be that way, what do I have to do to be that way? Early enough so you haven't built a defense mech-

92

anism to hide what you know, and also early enough so you really have time to work on changing."

"Kids that age couldn't answer that kind of question," says Tex.

"Well, I'm asking you."

"That's a hard one," he says.

"Then let's get back to the easier one. Why did you come here?"

"As I said, you know."

"Here's what I know," I say. "The reason you gave me was a lie. It had something to do with your mom. I don't—there are a bunch of things that contradict."

Wait, that phone call he made. . .

"The day we talked about *The Scream*. You called someone."

"So?" His poker face tells me I've hit some kind of target.

"Who did you call?"

"Why does it matter?"

"I know who you called," I say. "You called your mom."

He tries to keep his head still, I can see it, but he nods.

"Why?" I ask. "You called Doreen, what did you tell her?" My brain's racing, this matters to me. "You called her to say: the water's safe, come in."

"Wow," he says.

"You called to tell her it was OK for her to come here, didn't you? Am I crazy?"

"I did," he says. "As to whether you're crazy—"

"You called her to tell her it was safe to come here. I want to ask you what made you think so, but there's something more important. You called. . .you were her spy. She—my God, she sent you here. She sent you here to signal when it was safe to come. Is that it?"

Tex is looking down, debating. Is it something else?

I'm remembering someone claiming there are enlightened beings on the planet, folks who've meditated so deeply that they really have gotten past all the illusions. Is it true? Does the census bureau keep numbers? Which country has the highest ratio of enlightened beings to overall population?

"You don't want to tell me," I say.

"That's true," he says.

"I really want you to," I say.

Still he hesitates.

"Did I mention that I'm your father?"

"All right," he says. "Look, Mom was ill. She had a feeling I needed to make contact with you."

"For your sake."

"Yes, but also for yours."

"And for hers. That's the thing. For hers too. Am I right?"

"Yes," says Tex. "She was trying to complete things in her life before she died. And she felt that something special happened between you two. And if she went and it was too soon, completion wouldn't happen."

"Is she a reincarnationist? Wants to get the work done so it's better next time? Somebody did an efficiency study, make the most of your next incarnation?"

"It's not so much that," says Tex. "There's a Buddhist tale involving a strawberry."

"I know one about a mustard seed," I say. "A mother's despondent over her child dying, she goes to the Buddha, he tells her that she can bring back her child if she brings a mustard seed from a house whose family hasn't experienced death."

"In the one I'm thinking of," says Tex, "or at least the version I heard, a monk comes to a cliff, a tiger approaches, the monk stumbles over the edge, clings to a vine of strawberries, the vine's breaking, he'll fall to his death. Before he falls he tastes one of the strawberries and it's the most delicious strawberry he's ever had."

"And your Mom?"

"She wanted to taste that strawberry."

"A woman of the moment."

"She could savor the richness of the moment, yes," says Tex.

"I've never understood such things," I say.

"What things?"

"The only things of value are the permanent ones," I say. "That's why I was attracted to math."

"Why?"

"Why what?"

"Why must only permanent things have value?"

"I don't really know," I say. "It's just how I am."

"That's your monkey trap," he says. "Close your fist around—"

"I know about the monkey trap," I say. "Are you telling me she was holding on 'til she saw me?"

"Something like that," he says. "I'm not sure. Sometimes I just trust her. Trusted her." Sad-flooded eyes. Nice touch giving us tears, Creator.

We've hired a new cosmologist, he's a star, campus publicity decides he should pose with me. I like him so I strike up a conversation and he takes me on a tour of the universe.

"What's the difference for my life between Newton and Einstein?" I ask.

"Well, for one, Newton's English."

"I mean, the theories."

He thinks. Does other stuff too, a little digestion.

"Suppose tomorrow," he says, "the sun vanishes. How long until we feel the change in gravity?"

"How would the sun vanish?" I ask.

"Don't worry about that," he says.

"How can I not worry about the sun vanishing?"

"I'm just saying suppose," he says. "Under Newton, we'd feel it immediately because gravity is instantaneous. Under Einstein, it would take eight minutes because gravity travels at the speed of light."

"I prefer Einstein," I say. "Time to get in a quickie."

We sit quietly. I'm imagining this wave of disappearance slowly spreading from the vacated sun until it crashes against the Earth, wham.

"This may be out of your field," I say, "but those orbiting electrons, do they go in circles? Ellipses?"

"I'm not sure they're really orbits," he says. "Down at that level I don't even know if there's geometry."

"Why not?"

"Well, geometry requires space," he says. "And matter creates space, and at that level there isn't much matter to talk about. You're the Einstein of our age and you really never came upon this stuff?"

"Yes," I say.

Truth is, I've been a hungry reader since the broccolites first showed up. Tried to figure out the whole ball of wax, still trying, just very solitary about it. So when I don't know something I don't ask, makes for big gaps in my knowledge.

"Yes what?"

"Yes, I've read about it, I've read a few hundred books on quantum mechanics, started when I was eleven. Read the guys from the 1920s, and any time a new book gets a good review I make my way through."

He's happy. What is it with people?

"That makes more sense," he says, inhales deeply. "I mean, you're Quantum Biotechnics, for God's sake."

"Sense in what way?"

"Like when I learned of how many billions of neurons are in the brain, and how many possible connections that means."

"Because?"

"A brain so big, I can see how intelligence could fit in. Like having enough time explains evolution."

I tell Tex my fantasy about a cruel afterlife, our helplessness. He listens so kindly I can't believe he's my flesh and blood.

"It sounds like it's from your orphanhood," he says.

"How so?"

"Let's suppose that in the absence of love, life terrified you. Which is too much to bear, so you pretended it's a benevolent world, but deep down you never believed it. OK?"

"I don't know," I say.

"Your real feeling, your true perspective, keeps emerging and each time you mistake it for an aspect of existence itself."

"Come again?"

"What if you project the horror of your infancy onto the unknown, onto any unknown, the same way one can create a depressive state by thinking a sequence of depressive thoughts?"

"Maybe you're right," I say. "I feel it as you say it. But does that mean there's no hell?"

"I don't know," says Tex.

"Why don't you know?" I'm caught up in it, want him to have answers.

"I don't know what happens after death," he says. "But there's an identical story in several religions about the difference between heaven and hell."

"Which is?"

"Hell is a long table covered with food, all the billions who've gone there are seated on both sides, arms chained, all trying to eat but they can't reach their own mouths, though they can reach in almost every other direction."

"And heaven?"

"Heaven's the same except they're trying to feed each other."

I want to say something but my mind goes blank.

"There are so many questions we can get caught up in," says Tex, sneezing. "Maybe our thought just can't reach certain answers. I wish you'd have faith."

"Faith's a synonym for infancy," I say.

"You're sure about that?" asks Tex. "Have you looked at your own life closely? Have you studied how faith fits into other people's lives?"

"Faith in what?"

"In your case, faith that the world's not out to get you. A change in your basic view of what we're born into. Life includes suffering, yes, not your fault, and it's OK. So relax already, how about it Pops?"

It's all just words, what good are they?

The longest sleep of my life. I sleep through night and most of day. Around dinnertime I go for a walk. A girl approaches.

"They want you to talk," she says, pulling me by the arm, pretty coed, say eighteen.

"This isn't how to treat a professor," I say.

"They've gathered on the grass, and they want you to talk."

"You realize that if you weren't so pretty I'd be saying no."

She blushes a little.

"Oh come on," I say, "you knew that was why it would work."

A few hundred kids are gathered on the grass just waiting for me to talk. It must be one of those moments, I just meet a need. I remember when Mario Savio got on that car-roof at Berkeley.

They're all looking up at me.

"You want me to talk?" I ask.

"Just tell us," says the girl who dragged me.

I'm wondering what they need from me, and how I can avoid giving it to them. But there's innocence on that grass and the orphan within me is suddenly screaming: I need this, I need this, you who've run your life so stupidly, and I'm you.

"All right," I say. "But I don't know what you need me to say."

It's early evening, June, enough heat in the day that the bowl of campus and neighboring town, everything under the sky, is the perfect temperature as if inside and outside are merged, the whole day simmering to serve this moment.

"Just tell us," shouts a kid.

"What did you come to hear?" I ask.

"We came to hear the beauty-moment of spirituality," he shouts. "We came to be inspired."

I'm lost, even scared. Screw with them, sure, but somehow—

A new idea enters my mind.

"Suppose we go one by one," I say. "Starting there, at the far left. Each of you, tell me what makes you most sure that you're really living your life, as opposed to something someone else created?"

"Starting with me?"

"Yes."

"I don't know what to say."

"Take your time," I say. "Just be honest."

A pause and then she's saying it, and one by one they stand and speak, telling what's most genuine in their existence, an awed hush over the field, our sacred experience.

"That's what I came to tell you," I lie. "That feeling we all have right now."

"Did you really?" asks the girl that dragged me. "You are magical."

I can't lie to her, something in me...

"No," I say. "I didn't. It came from all of you. And at this moment I do love all of you, and this is the least alone I've ever felt in my life."

"We want to know it all," shouts a kid I know, real shy, must be real need.

"And what exactly is it that you want to know?"

"We want to know what's ahead for us," he says.

"I don't know that," I say.

"But that isn't really it," he says. "We want to know if everything's gonna be OK. Or if everything is OK. Will we love our children right? Will we find happiness? Will the world disappoint or crush us?"

"We want to know," shouts another kid, "if you can find your happiness that we all wish for you."

"For me? Why me?"

"Because if anyone has it, you have it. You've won the biggest lottery. You're a benefactor to millions."

Must be a giant con, they've brought me to my moment of deepest wish just to humiliate me, mock me. I'm so close to—

I'm crying, doubled over with tears, and the girl who dragged me comes and stands before me and puts her arms around me, and people are crying all across the field, and I didn't know such a thing was possible.

"It's OK," she's saying. "It's OK." Cradles me, rocks me in her arms.

I close my eyes tighter and cry harder and I hear her soft voice in my ears, reassurance I never had and it all fits, what I was waiting for all my life, all my life. I must have cried for fifteen minutes, who knew there was so much water in me?

"No one has moved, no one has left," she says, as if reading my mind.

Now what do I do?

And again she seems to read my mind, how does she know, is it a need so basic that you can know this about someone else, back before cities, protoplasmic urges?

"Nothing to do," she says. "Nothing, nothing to do."

I tell Jume what happened on the field.

"Yes," she says. "I heard. Everybody's heard."

"I can't believe it," I say. "I cried."

"I heard that too."

What Jume said to me that was so upsetting was that the broccolites might be my way of allowing another side of me to come out—might not really be there. That's what made me want to strangle her. I decide to talk about it

"Why was it so upsetting?" she asks. I notice she's a little further back from the computer than usual.

"I have no idea," I say.

"Let's think about this logically," she says.

"Suppose you do that," I say. "I'll be waiting here."

"This is a process that involves us both," she says.

"All right," I say. "Do we start with Aristotelian logic, or do we go entirely symbolic, go with Boole?"

"I'm gonna take that as a cry for help," she says.

"So where's the help?"

"What if these impulses,," she asks, "are really a side of you? What would it mean to you if there's a side of you that runs the universe—"

"The whole ball of wax?"

"Well, I really mean your universe, life as you experience and live it."

In a sudden blind rage I slam the computer shut way too hard and there's a sound no laptop owner wants to hear. But in that instant I feel something new, with an inner vision I notice something new: beneath my rage is something else, a different feeling.

I ask around. What can you do if you realize you're seeking something harmful to yourself and doing so because it has a connection to something so powerful? Somebody must know, right?

Let's try Rhyth.

"Interesting you should ask," says Rhyth.

"Why?"

"I have a project," says Rhyth. He's devoting his life to figuring out why things are going so badly for humanity, all the ideas he can find, just thinking.

"Anything you can suggest for the time being?" I ask.

"It could start with the Internet," he says. "A slow planet-wide—"

"I mean, for me specifically."

Alan Salant *Ablong*

"Oh, that's harder," he says, and I swear to God, I don't know how to take it.

"How's your new laptop?" asks Jume.

"So far so good. And the warranty covers destruction due to therapy."

"Ready to talk more about the broccolites?"

"I guess," I say. "I don't know what to make of them."

"View them psychoanalytically."

"Meaning?"

"View your life as a work of art. What do the broccolites stand for?"

"I get the feeling they're rather intolerant," I say, "a short fuse, so they wouldn't stand for a whole lot."

"I mean, what do they represent in you? What aspects of you?"

A thousand thoughts enter my mind but I keep them to myself, don't even want to write them down.

I'm watching my broccolites from a different angle, and something makes me shiver. They're what?—dinosaurs, gigantic mouths. No, worse, giant worms. No, chromosomes. No, not chromosomes either.

They're something else, and I get this feeling of the implacable vastness of the universe.

Tex takes Ed aside. I eavesdrop.

"You don't have to take it," he says. OK, he's trying again to fix Ed. The first time looked like it might work, but Ed backslid.

"Take what?" asks Ed.

"The abuse. The constant abuse from my Dad."

"Ah, it's nothing," says Ed.

"It's abuse," says Tex.

"Maybe he abuses you," says Ed. "He doesn't abuse me."

I could have predicted from general principles that Ed would get angry at Tex, surprised Tex didn't see it coming.

"He has nothing to offer you," says Tex. "There's nothing in it for you. Take away his power by realizing that."

"You're just like him," says Ed.

If that's true, my work here is done. And that's what Tex came here for. I'm curious about his next move.

"Look, Ed," says Tex.

"I'd prefer to be called Professor Blumenthal," says Ed.

I know what I'd do with that, but it stops Tex. Well, he's still just a kid.

"Sorry, Professor Blumenthal," says Tex after a minute. "But just imagine another person. Call him Joe. Joe has unmet needs from infancy, nothing unusual in that. He looks to satisfy them, nothing unusual in that either. He goes to a place where they can't be met. And that isn't unusual either."

"And?"

"If Joe would only be kind to himself, if he'd see what he really needs—and there are people who help with that—he'd be happier. And Joe doesn't exactly seem to be dying of happiness. And he's a real nice guy who deserves to be happy. Really."

"I do understand that this fictional Joe is meant to be me, but he isn't me," says Ed, though something's a bit softer in him.

"Why do you think," asks Tex, "that my Dad attributes these stories to you? Why do you think these ideas even enter his mind? Because they're part of him, expressing him, in a way he hasn't yet become calm enough to accept as himself. But he will, and when he does they'll be the material of his rebuilding. And Joe's also my Dad, though my Dad's Joe may be buried deeper than yours. Hear that, Pops?"

I have to pretend I don't. And no, my work isn't done here yet. Tex is a good guy.

"I'm ready to move on," says Tex.

"What do you mean?"

"I got what I need from you," he says. "I'm whole, father-wise. I'm ready to move on."

He's already packed.

"But you're not an asshole."

"Turns out that's not what I needed from you."

By afternoon he's gone. That evening I realize, first time in my life I let myself feel it, that I'm lonely.

So I invite women. First up's a Proust scholar who's just discovered Joyce, excited they both wrote masterworks that end back at the beginning. Oh, the turf wars ahead...

"*A Skeleton Key* to *Finnegans Wake*," she says post-coitally, "tells of the detailed description of the descent of spirit into space and time. I imagined a different kind of book."

"Like a graphic novel?"

That puzzles her for a moment.

"Not necessarily," she says. "It would say the sorts of things medieval scholars said, except this time they'd be simple descriptions demonstrable by repeatable experiment. Someone with a justifiable self-confidence telling it like it is, explaining the whole universe, psyche and all. Not only is it all knowable, it's all known, and now it's a question of getting in tight with—"

"With a good librarian."

"Exactly," she says. "You know, what they say about you isn't true. You're a good listener, and you're kind of sweet. I feel like I can tell you anything and you'll understand. Truth be told, I can't stand being with stupid guys."

"I'm touched by your perceptiveness," I say. "And I have precisely the same trouble with stupid guys."

Lester comes by to see how I'm doing, Lizbeth's at a conference. Sent to me by Tex, no doubt.

"How's it hanging?" he asks.

"To answer that," I say, "I'd need to know which particular 'it' we're discussing. Also precisely what aspects of its hanging are in question."

"Let me rephrase it," says Lester.

"I'm afraid I can't allow that," I say.

"How are you?" he asks.

It occurs to me to say how lonely I feel. But injured animals know not to limp, nature pounces on weakness. How do they know? Some collection of nerve cells in the 'on' position. Passed down generations?

"I'm fine," I say. No limp.

"Good," he says. "OK if I sleep in the guest room tonight?"

"You're asking?" All those other times...

He smiles with a trace of embarrassment and I wish I hadn't said it that way, I'm so happy not to be alone.

"Is it OK?"

"Yes," I say.

Around midnight I'm up, reading Proust backwards in the living room. Lester comes out.

"How's it really going?" he asks.

"I miss Tex," I say, didn't mean to.

"You're an orphan, right?"

I put down my Proust, very slowly.

"How could you possibly know? Is this some kind of orphan-to-orphan telepathy?"

"I can't put my finger on it," he says. "I just know."

"Does Tex?"

"I don't think so."

"Things just get worse with time," I say, no idea where that's coming from. "Slowly the forms of night are taking over the day."

"What do you mean?"

"Year by year the helplessness and the strange impossibilities of the night are being re-created in the day—by us, by us, by us. Our night minds are winning. History is the slow transfer of the darkness into the light."

"In what ways?"

"Kafkaesque spaces that stretched across Soviet years, or our jungle cities, the death we blow across the planet. But we don't witness the birth of these grotesque forms. Despite spiritual disciplines and the sacred therapist's couch we're mere tourists instead of citizens of the night. You know what we think?"

"What?"

"That we still aren't safe, but maybe tomorrow..."

"And?"

"A hundred thousand years from now we'll still be waging wars in the outside world against the demons of our own minds."

"Nah," says Lester, "we'll have been replaced by robots long before then. Anyway, what was it like for you?"

"What?"

"You know what."

"Are we doing an orphans' support group now?"

"What was it like?"

"It really sucked," I say.

"I know," he says.

"And it may surprise you to learn that I wasn't well liked," I say.

"That is a shocker," he admits.

"On my eighth birthday," I say, "kids locked me in a dark room. Luckily I always carried a small flashlight. There was a dictionary in the room, the only book, and I read it 'til my eyes strained, slowly realized how our abstract words are built on body, on material things, and it got me thinking."

"About what?"

"About how I couldn't figure out how the world works, like it was being lived in a language other people knew. And if I could understand the origins of the words, I could figure out what they knew that I didn't. String them together and I'd understand what's going on at a bar, a ballgame, a boardroom."

"I know the feeling," he says.

"You?" I say. "You seem part of the mix."

"In appearance only," says Lester. "You'd be surprised how many of us are alienated."

"By us, you mean orphans?"

"By us I mean humans."

"I sometimes wonder," I say, "if there's a book that tells all the words from which the social world is built, how the key categories of thought grow from the original language, core philology."

"What else did you think in that room?"

"What do you mean?"

"I mean, what was the real thing you thought in that room?"

I try to hide fear that surprises me in my eyes.

"Out with it," he says.

"That it was right that they locked me in the room. That I deserved it. That I belonged."

Lester goes to the refrigerator and gets two beers and we drink silently. Then we're discussing our empty unparented places of pain, the rhythms of isolation, talking for hours 'til Lester goes into the guest room and drops to sleep just as the sun's coming up.

I try an economist. She's super-saturated adulthood, says we're all rational, poor folk have only themselves to blame. Makes me feel inadequate but the Viagra holds.

I advance the notion of a God who's doing his best, the good-enough Creator.

"What are you talking about?" she asks.

"Have you noticed there's evil in the world?

"Yes."

"So what if it isn't that there's a deeper meaning to it, except that God really just did His best?"

"Blaming God is for weaklings," she says. "All blame is. If a person takes full responsibility for his life he sees why things are as they are."

"Where did you get your feminectomy done?" I ask. "Is there a particular doctor, or is it a clinic, or maybe one of those health mega-liths?"

She's the exact opposite of Doreen. OK, that's why I was so angry at her.

"You have a choice, she says. "You can attack my femininity, or you can, well, enjoy my femininity."

I think a minute.

"Come here," I say.

For weeks I feel the loneliness. Finally I just need Tex, I pick up as remembrance a book he gave me as a gift, *Dibs in Search of Self*, only gift he ever gave me, at least the only material one.

A slip of paper falls out. Digits: I'll bet it's his cell phone number.

"How did you get this number?" he asks.

"It fell out of the book you gave me."

"I am the master of the human universe," he says.

"What do you mean?"

"I mean, I got one right, Mom would've been proud. I figured when you really needed me, you'd take out that book—that's why I only gave you one present, ever—and you'd find my number. That way I'd avoid the intermediate bullshit."

"There are so many ways that could have gone wrong," I say.

"But it didn't. Anything else you want to say to me?"

"I want us to be in touch," I say. "A phone call now and then. Maybe even a webcam so we can see each other, that would be so nice."

"You got it, Pops," he says, and in that moment I realize that my anger's gone, this diary's done, this problem solved. There's a fruit stand nearby, I might go out for some strawberries.

Alan Salant *Ablong*